A low sigh of male satisfaction left his throat when Therin straightened and drew Kianti snug against his chest

Resting against the side of the piano, he deepened the kiss, thrusting his tongue slowly yet unrelentingly.

Kianti's hands kneaded his forearms and biceps, to test the strength beneath the dark fabric of his shirt. She moaned in the midst of suckling his tongue. Arching closer and rubbing herself against him in shameless abandon, she cursed the dress covering her skin.

Back off, Therin told himself, but he chose to set aside the order for a few seconds. He wanted longer to indulge in just a bit more of her. The serenity she radiated took on a more potent aura during their second kiss. He had no intention of stopping it.

The sound of her soft, helpless yet deliberate moans sent the strength right from his legs, causing him to lean more fully into the piano.

Kianti shuddered and snuggled deeper into the embrace as she assumed a more controlling role in the duel being fought between their tongues. She gripped his shirt as though it were her lifeline while inhaling the appealing scent of his cologne. There was that familiar voice in her head still singing its same old song. It told her to end this, but how could she when *this* was so sweet and so dearly missed....

Books by AlTonya Washington

Kimani Romance

A Lover's Pretense
A Lover's Mask
Pride and Consequence
Rival's Desire
Hudsons Crossing
The Doctor's Private Visit
As Good as the First Time
Every Chance I Get
Private Melody

ALTONYA WASHINGTON

wears many titles. Aside from Mom, her favorite is romance author. Crafting stories and characters that are sexy and engaging with a fair amount of mystery really keeps her busy. When AlTonya's not writing, she works as a library assistant and as social secretary to an active son—a job that commands the bulk of her time.

Private Melody

AlTonya Washington

KIMANI
ROMANCE

To the teachers who care, listen and communicate.
You know who you are.

 KIMANI PRESS™

ISBN-13: 978-0-373-86226-9

Recycling programs
for this product may
not exist in your area.

PRIVATE MELODY

Copyright © 2011 by AlTonya Washington

www.kimanipress.com

Printed in U.S.A.

Dear Reader,

Thanks for adding *Private Melody* to your collection. For a while now, I've been thinking of crafting a story where the subplot involves education. If you know my work, you know I love mixing in a fair amount of suspense and danger in addition to steamy romance and cozy settings. I'm really excited by what this mix has created.

In addition to this intriguing mix, I also had thoughts of creating a heroine with health concerns. I didn't want her to come across as a victim, but as a courageous woman surrounded by people who adore her, including an amazing man who is in awe of her. Of course she'd be fairly hardheaded, making her a challenge to her friends and irresistible to our sexy hero.

I hope you'll enjoy the results. Thanks for taking time to settle in for a *Private Melody.*

Blessings,

AlTonya
www.lovealtonya.com
altonya@lovealtonya.com

Chapter 1

Spokane, Washington

*P*rovocative, Powerful, Pulsating... Therin Rucker thought he'd puke after reading the *program* and finding it riddled by a slew of *P*s boasting of pianist Kianti Lawrence. He supposed the creators of the gold-edged publication thought it was all in good *promoting.* He shook his head to clear his thoughts. Perhaps it was simply the current state of his mood that lent to his opinion of the accolades aimed at the woman on the stage. Over the course of the last twenty minutes, however, his negative opinions had changed.

Fist propped to chin, Therin could feel his gaze narrowing as it focused more intently upon the gleaming hardwood stage set beneath the soft gold lighting. Uncontrolled, a low sound rose from his throat. Therin was aware that the sound was one of appreciation.

Whether that appreciation was in reference to the woman's exquisite talent or her exquisite looks was something Therin refused to dwell on even for a moment.

Vaughn Burgess thought differently and slanted his best friend a glance while a smirk crinkled his gaze. Therin's set expression was easy to read—for Vaughn, anyway. He'd seen the look often enough to know Therin was captivated—not so much by the music as by the woman performing it.

Therin switched his stance, propping his chin against the opposite fist. His crystalline hazel stare lost none of its intensity.

The charity concert for the Pacific Northwest political organization EYES—Educate Youth Encourage Success—was for a worthy cause and one close to Therin's heart. However, he'd have much preferred diving right into the heart of the matter at hand instead of sitting through a piano recital. That was before he took his seat and had his attention and…other things captivated by the lovely artist in his midst.

The performance was nearing its conclusion. After the final stanza was complete, Therin lent his attention to the room. Despite the unexpected musical treat, he knew his evening wouldn't end on a high note.

It was wildly rumored that the money funneled into the EYES organization could claim standing in the high nine figures. EYES was certainly a force to be reckoned with and it made good on its promises. While the EYES organization held the noblest intentions, there were those who would have preferred its influential members spend their time and considerable wealth on other endeavors.

The applause was deafening in the Hotel Currey's concert hall. There were even chants for an encore. Kianti Lawrence laughed vibrantly while raising her hands to wave off the requests.

Therin didn't leave his seat right away. Tugging at the crisp white cuffs peeking out from his tuxedo jacket sleeve, he merely observed the scene. The smile on his face then was more rueful than amused. If only the crowd there could come together in agreement over situations more prevalent....

No, the evening would not end on a high note. Many in that room held similar opinions on the way he spent his time, money...and resources. They thought it out of place for the young American ex-ambassador to Canada to hold such a topic as education as his passion. Therin's dedication and his almost magical ability to sway influential friends to dedicate themselves toward the same purpose had earned him an almost equal number of enemies.

Kianti gave one last low curtsy and prayed that her legs wouldn't give out from beneath her. Silently, she sent up other prayers of thanks that the audience couldn't see her legs shaking beneath the floor-length hemline of her gown. She left the group with her customary double wave and almost sprinted from the stage.

She kept the smile pasted to her mouth until all other smiling faces were left behind. She only needed a moment—just a moment—to get herself together. Brody would have a pill down her throat fast if she didn't make herself scarce. She didn't need that. She never wanted to need *that* again.

"I need to go." Therin said the words almost to himself.

Vaughn heard him clearly. "'Bout damn time you get your mind on somethin' other than work."

Therin shrugged and refused to make eye contact with his friend. "Calm down, V, just goin' to the john."

"Uh-huh."

The guys stood in unison. Therin couldn't maintain the pretense for long and grinned at Vaughn's knowing glare. His stare had softened, although his light eyes began to scan the noisy room.

"Keep 'em off my back for five minutes, V." He shook hands with Vaughn and moved on.

Kianti shivered, and not from the backstage breeze that kissed her shoulder through the black lacy sleeves of her gown. In her world, there were only small windows of chance to happen upon unclaimed spaces at concert halls. During the last seven years of her professional career, she'd been blessed to catch those "windows" open after almost every performance.

As the audience conversed among themselves—shuffling from their seats and remarking on the talent they'd just witnessed and how it compared to others—Kianti sought that time to collect herself and to catch her breath.

She never wanted to need *that* again....

Therin cursed Vaughn below his breath, but realized, in all fairness, the man was probably elsewhere working to give him his requested "five minutes." Unfortunately, his chief of staff couldn't be everywhere at once, Therin grudgingly admitted. He worked up a fake smile for the group of Capitol Hill policymakers who waited along his path.

"Heard it through the grapevine Therin—you're thinking of arranging a week-long retreat at your Vancouver place," Jonas Dessin commented once the group made quick work of handshakes and small talk. "Rumor has it, it's another EYES fundraiser."

Therin laughed, clapping Jonas's arm. "Does your grapevine have any idea what EYES's bottom line is? Last thing they need is another fundraiser."

"Grapevine also says it's a membership drive," Susan Brunschwig noted once the laughter had settled over Therin's last comment.

He shrugged, his demeanor cool in the face of the subtle yet pointed inquiries. It wasn't difficult. He'd been playing politics since he was four.

Stepping closer to Susan, Therin kept his smile light even as hers broadened and the stiff set to her body softened. "Education is in a precarious state." He spared the woman's colleagues a fleeting glance but directed his remark to her. "It was in an even worse condition before EYES came on the scene. We have a damn hard battle to fight. The kids we're fighting for will need every able body we can find to take on this battle. So yes, Susan, membership is always in need. Good night all." He bid smoothly and walked on.

Jonas Dessin turned to follow Therin's exit. "There goes a dangerous young man."

Susan kept her eyes on Therin heading deeper into the crowd. "Why dangerous, Jonas?"

"That kind of money going toward education? Are you kidding me?" Jonas's eyes crinkled at the corners.

"It may not be so far-fetched."

"That's true—hence the young man being a danger. He's rattling folks that would have the big amounts he woos from his...*members* go toward other endeavors— endeavors far removed from education. EYES boasts a powerful and prominent membership list and every one of those members loves that young man. Those un- sympathetic to his cause are threatened by that." Jonas took a breather from his diatribe and helped himself to a drink off the tray of a passing waiter. "Like I said, there goes a dangerous young man."

The serene backstage moment lasted longer than Kianti dared to hope it would. She even had time to kick up her heels. Literally. She'd pulled a chair closer to the one she occupied and propped up her feet. *May as well make the most of it,* she thought. Any minute the vultures would descend.

Kianti felt a smile emerge and quietly chastised her- self. She loved her career and the madness that often came with it. Though there were varied aspects she could have done without, the greatest share of it had been a blessing.

Those who loved and followed her work had grown into a staggering number in the seven years since the start of her career. She was still in awe of it. She'd always been modest about her talents, even as a child, when she started playing the tune her mother hummed while preparing dinner one evening. It was a crude rendition of the melody banged out on Kianti's pink toy piano, but it was enough to give her parents pause.

Not long after, the then four-year-old Kianti learned the word "prodigy." Her parents and all the new teachers they brought in were talking about her when they said it. Those days had long passed, but even now she found it difficult to believe how taken aback people were when they discovered what she could do with a piano.

To herself, she would admit to succumbing to a bit of smugness over it. The more awestruck people were, the more she was allowed to do what she loved. In spite of the fact that she put her life at stake every time she did it.

Therin found her in a remote corner backstage. He sighed. It was not until then that he realized he'd been holding his breath. She'd been taking deep breaths as well, he noted, appreciating the fact that her eyes were closed. His presence was not yet noticed. No doubt she'd be unnerved and rightly agitated finding some stranger intruding on her private moment.

Her music was enchanting, but he wouldn't lie that it was more than her talent that had him rushing backstage to find her. Part of him wondered if it was all about her looks, either. After all, he'd been seated too far away to focus in on every nuance of her very lovely face. He wasn't surprised to find her as captivating at a distance as she was once that distance was closed.

Cinnamon-brown and fine-boned, she appeared doll-like and far too fragile to pound out the driving rhythms that she gave less than an hour ago. Her eyes appeared to tilt at the corners and he wondered at their color, but didn't want her opening her eyes just yet. He needed more time to observe, and it was then that he recognized what he was seeking when he disappeared backstage to find her.

There was calm, a serenity that he'd swear was almost visible. It followed her and he wanted it or…at least a moment to enjoy whatever part of it she might unknowingly share.

He watched as she reached up to finger the glittering band that held her coarse dark hair away from her face. She opened her eyes then and looked right at him as if she'd been aware of his presence all along. Along with the cool expectancy in her bottomless dark stare, there was also the hint of curiosity.

"I'm sorry."

His first words sparked a smile and a slight indentation along her left cheek that hinted at a dimple.

"What for?" she asked.

Therin took a moment, long brows rising slightly as he regarded his answer. He'd known the reason for the apology but when she asked, his mind went completely blank. What the hell was wrong with him? He prayed she hadn't detected the frown he was trying to hide.

Kianti tilted her head and observed him. A lost tourist, perhaps? She'd detected a chord in the two words he'd spoken. Something old-world or, at the very least, regal, clung to his tone.

"I wanted to compliment your playing," he said after a quick swallow and clearing of his throat. "Phenomenal." He grimaced over the word choice.

Her nod was barely there, yet her smile was genuine. "Thank you."

Therin risked a glance down the narrow corridor leading back toward the main stage. Hands hidden in the deep pockets of his black pants, he moved closer to where she lounged.

"The pamphlet they're passing around mentioned that you play by ear."

"It's true." She shrugged. "If I had a piano near, you could hum a tune and I'd prove it."

Laughter rumbled easy and soft between them.

"Therin Rucker." He extended one of the hidden hands he'd pulled from his pocket.

She accepted the shake. "Kianti Lawrence."

His sleek brows rose again. "Like the wine?"

"Not quite." She grinned. "Pronounced the same, but spelled differently. Many people tell me I'm much harder to take than the wine."

The sound of voices growing nearer intruded on their second round of laughter. Kianti promptly eased her hand out of Therin's grasp.

"Here she is, y'all!"

Kianti gave a short laugh as she often did when Cube David's voice reached her ears. However, she'd hoped for just a few more moments with the mysterious music lover who'd just introduced himself.

Unfortunately, the three men following Cube made their presence known all too soon. Thankfully, they stifled any questions when they discovered her with "company."

"Therin Rucker, Cube David—my bodyguard." She made the introductions, still seated with her feet up.

"Winton Terry—my business manager. Khan Choi is my stylist and this is Brody Parker my—uh—cook."

Someone snickered and Brody's mouth tightened.

Kianti didn't attempt to hide her surprise or confusion when all four of her associates approached Therin for handshakes. They all grinned broadly and addressed her mysterious "music lover" as Mr. Ambassador, which roused a curious frown between her brows. She watched Therin chuckle as he engaged in light conversation with the guys.

She used the time to more closely observe him. She'd been trying like the devil not to gawk when she'd opened her eyes and found him standing there. Leanly muscular and quite tall, she doubted even the chic pumps she wore would prevent her from having to look up into his face. And what a face it was, every square inch of it drenched in a flawless cinnamon-brown. Then there were the long sideburns, which added a dangerous but nonetheless provocative appeal to his features. His hair was cut close and lay in waves of silky black over his head. She could have lost herself in the crystal appearance of his hazel gaze deep set beneath long, heavy brows.

"Well, we appreciate you attending tonight," Khan was saying as the conversation began to taper off.

Winton chuckled. "Yeah, even if you *are* here to conduct top-secret political business."

Contagious male laughter rumbled once more.

"Not so top secret," Therin admitted while pressing a thumb to his eye to remove a laugh tear. "Anyway, I'm glad I attended, too." His shimmering gaze focused on Kianti then. "Ms. Lawrence's music is…quite powerful.

It was nice meeting you." His tone grew softer as he reached out to shake hands with the guys and say good-night.

Alone with Kianti, the guys pulled chairs close. Brody claimed the closest spot and took her wrist for a pulse check.

"We leave you alone for a second and here you are meeting with royalty," Khan noted while fluffing out her hair.

Kianti's gaze and attention was still on the path Therin Rucker had taken when he made his exit.

Chapter 2

Therin woke early the next morning and was thoroughly agitated shortly afterward. The staff and their discussions that he had to shake off last night had descended upon his suite with their opinions of the previous evening.

"He stirred up a shitload of crap just by attending that thing," Vaughn said while he helped himself to coffee from the breakfast cart.

"Put himself smack dab in the middle of some heavy hitters, that's for sure," Peter Stanson added while waving toward Vaughn for the carafe.

"Yeah, heavy hitters who either approve or oppose EYES and the ex-ambassador's allegiance to it." Chief of security, Morgan Felts, muttered a curse while stretching out on the cream sofa in the living area.

Therin predicted the conversation among his top three staff members would only grow more heated. For a change, he welcomed that. Hopefully, their discussion would keep his absence from being noticed for a while. He slipped out the suite without alerting their attention.

For a *long* while, he corrected himself upon arriving in the almost empty breakfast bistro located in the hotel mezzanine. Finding Kianti Lawrence there had him regretting that any shred of business had followed him along on the trip.

He thought back to the previous evening, recalling his loss of words when she'd first spoken to him. The sensible, less popular side of his demeanor told him to leave her alone. There was no need to grow more infatuated than he'd already become in the span of the ten-minute conversation with the woman. The only thing further "involvement" could result in was a one-night stand. That wouldn't work for him—he knew that without question. Kianti Lawrence was a woman he was certain to want for more than one night.

He was surprised to find Kianti already having breakfast. Leaning against the arched doorway of the hotel's eatery, he felt content watching her then as he had the night before. Almost. The same serenity and calm reached out to him from where she relaxed at the table across the dining room. He shook his head and smiled, taking note of her feet propped in the chair across from where she sat. He couldn't help but admire her determination to relax wherever it suited her. Telling the sensible, less popular side of himself to go to hell, Therin pushed off the doorway and strolled toward her.

Early rising wasn't unusual for Kianti given her hectic life of tours and rehearsals. Still, she did make a point of treating herself to a few mornings of sleeping in when she traveled extensively.

Sadly, sleeping in now meant having to wake up to her doctor and a morning pill. An early breakfast meant she could convince Brody she'd already taken her meds. She only prayed he wouldn't suspect she'd taken herself off them. At least not until she could prove she didn't need them anymore. Her dark eyes were focused beyond the windows by her table. The gorgeous dewy morning rear view of the hotel landscape was heavenly, but the cologne drifting past her nose just then was to die for. She smiled up at Therin.

"Mr. Ambassador." Her dark eyes widened just slightly when she took note of the shyness evident in his expression.

"Ex-ambassador," he clarified, pressing a hand to the front of the sweatshirt emblazoned with the Knicks logo.

She simply shrugged. "But you never quite live it down, do you?"

Once again that morning, Therin felt his mouth turn into a grimace. "I'm realizing that more and more every day." He sighed.

Kianti's smile waned. She'd never really known a politician, but it was clear this one wasn't missing his post all that much. She would have loved to have known why.

"You look pretty young to have been an ambassador." She decided to keep the moment light.

"Guess I've got my dad to thank for that. May I?" He gestured toward the vacant chair next to the one she'd propped her feet on.

"Please." She was about to move her feet when he brought a hand down over them. Kianti bit her lip and stilled.

The muscle flexed in Therin's jaw at the contact. He moved his hand, hoping she'd not recognize his reluctance to do so.

"So your dad wanted you to be an ambassador?" She needed to bring conversation to the front of her mind instead of the unexpected agitating throbs that made her want to moan.

"My dad was a U.S. diplomat," Therin obliged, needing the conversation, as well. "When I was a kid, watching *Face The Nation* was as commonplace as watching *Sesame Street.*"

"Fascinating," Kianti breathed, shifting a bit to get more comfy at the table.

Therin must have feared she'd move her feet because he possessively dropped his hand across them. They were small, perfectly proportioned and covered only by a pair of sheer hose.

"I had a capacity for politics but not a passion," he confided while absently applying a light massage to the tops of her feet. "I think they offered me the post because of my father." He grunted. "I'd have never campaigned for it or anything else."

"So the favorite son makes good."

"Ha! More like the *only* son."

"Well, well, pleased to meet another member of the Only Child Club." Kianti offered him her hand to shake.

Therin played along. "So your parents didn't want to try for another musical genius?"

"Nah." Kianti fidgeted with the draping neckline

of her walnut-brown sweater. "My mother didn't have a—how did you put it?—a *capacity* for raising more than one. Besides, it wasn't worth it to her—taking the chance of producing a normal kid."

Therin's bright eyes narrowed at her word choice, but there was no time to inquire.

"Please forgive the wait, Mr. Ambassador." The waiter was flushed and out of breath.

"Not a problem. Just juice and whatever Ms. Lawrence is having."

"Yes, sir." The young man scribbled the order furiously. "Right away, sir."

"I feel like such an idiot." Kianti shook her head and watched the server sprint away. "Everyone knows who you are and I didn't have a clue."

"And you have no idea how pleased I am to hear that." He cast a disinterested glance across his shoulder and smirked. "Besides, they school the staff on the so-called 'big wigs.' Better tips, you know?" He winked.

When she threw her head back to laugh, Therin decided he was in need of conversation to keep the moment from growing too charged. "So why do you consider yourself other than normal?" he asked.

"Well, prodigies aren't exactly the norm, are they?" Kianti rested her chin to her palm.

He nodded, realizing her point. "Hard life?"

"I suppose." She studied the pattern embroidered into the white tablecloth. "But what are you gonna do? It's the only life I've ever known—didn't know any better until I had something to compare it to." She fixed him with a whimsical look. "Kids playing in the street while I'm in the house playing Bach."

Laughter rose heartily then.

"So may I question your 'only son' remark?" she probed once the waiter had brought out Therin's juice and topped off her decaf.

"Mmm." He winced while taking a sip of the drink. "Was hoping you hadn't caught that."

"Come on, fess up." She waved her hands in a beckoning manner. "It's only fair. I rarely share my child prodigy stories." Her gaze softened as she studied the pensive look on his very handsome face. "Did you regret not having brothers or sisters?"

"Maybe, but it's the only life I've known—nothing to compare it to, as you said."

"Touché." Kianti sent him a mock salute.

Food arrived and soon the two were dining on over-easy eggs, steak strips and toast.

"Guess that's why I took up the interests I have," Therin said around a bite of steak.

Kianti nodded. "Politics."

He smiled. "Education."

She tilted her head at a cocky angle. "Now you've really got me interested. Talk, man!"

They dived into the incredible breakfast of fruit, seasoned browns and scrambled eggs. Seated next to an enviable view in a peaceful dining room they chatted like longtime acquaintances.

"Growing up...*privy* to dedicated teachers and fine schools made me naively think *that* was the norm," he shared. "Then I realized that too many parents, and kids, for that matter, wouldn't put *dedicated* teachers and *fine* schools together in the same book. It made me sick to my stomach." He held his fork poised over the plate and glared out at the view. "No child should be denied a fine education, and no parent should feel it's beyond their power to claim it for their child."

Silently, Kianti marveled how there could be any education woes with a man like the one seated across from her as its champion.

Therin noticed her set expression and closed his eyes in playful regret. "Sorry about that." He tapped the tip of the fork to the cleft in his chin. "I tend to get carried away." His voice lowered an octave on the last word.

"That's not it." She waved off the excuse. "You're very persuasive in your arguments. My guess is that you're a fundraiser's dream."

"Hmph." Therin returned his attention to breakfast and didn't appear to appreciate the assessment. "So I've been told," he grumbled.

"Did I offend you?"

"No, Kianti." He tapped his fingers next to her plate and waited for her eyes to meet his. "No. I've just got a lot of friends and…acquaintances who tell me the same thing. Many times they don't mean to flatter me with it."

"Well, that's crazy. What could be more admirable than taking up such a cause?"

He smiled at the innocence he'd once been a victim of. "Kianti, everything pales next to the cause of raking in obscene amounts of cash for the next war."

"Ah." Enlightenment dawned and she nodded. "So is that why you gave up your ambassadorship? To devote more time to your cause?" she asked, following several moments of easy silence.

"One of many reasons," was his only reply. His

thoughts drifted toward his parents. His involvement—er—obsession over his cause had cut short that relationship far too soon. At least, he had always suspected that was the case.

Kianti caught his grimace again and decided to call a halt to the Q&A.

"Someone once told me that with power comes the ability to make change in addition to suggestion," he eventually added somewhat prophetically.

"I've always thought of ambassadors and such as figureheads. Sorry," she said demurely before sipping her coffee. She was pleased to hear him chuckle.

"You're not too far off." He helped himself to his last forkful of eggs. "As ambassador, I found that I could suggest 'til the cows came home, but *affecting* change—" he brushed the back of his hand along a sideburn "—affecting change eluded me until I left my post."

"You left your post yet you remain in Vancouver? No desire to return home to the States?" A teasing element made her eyes sparkle.

Therin shrugged. "Canada's not so far away. I'm in the States off and on. But I really like where I am—many diplomats aren't so lucky."

Kianti added a bit more cream to her coffee. "It would seem you could do more for the cause on *this* side of the border, that's all."

"Well, that's what's so impressive about the organization." Therin settled in more comfortably. "We're everywhere. EYES members and branch offices across the country go a long way to give the impression that we're a strong united group. Everyone works equally hard which is another reason we're so successful." He thanked the waiter who'd returned with a fresh glass of juice. "Education's my passion, and while I've been labeled as the *face* of EYES, I'm not its leader. That's a joint responsibility."

"It's a different outlook." Kianti studied his very handsome face with unmasked appreciation. "Guess the opposition doesn't quite know how to take you all."

Therin chuckled, causing his provocative gaze to narrow. "I think that'd be the case no matter who we were. Politics is a nasty game. You have to be…creative to get things done."

"I see…creative here being akin to corrupt?" she guessed.

He raised his juice glass. "Smart lady."

Kianti shrugged. "Things aren't much different in the music world."

"Yet you remain a faithful contributor?"

It was her turn to mull over a response. "I feel an obligation to continue. There're a lot of talented kids out there but this is not an easy business to break into. Instrumental performing—piano, orchestra, symphonies—there's a fair amount of politics at play and getting your shot isn't always as easy as knowing how to play the hell out of an instrument." She smiled but there was little humor in the gesture. "Many kids have the raw talent," she extended her hand, "and nowhere to cultivate it. No proper *pedigree,* if you get my meaning."

Therin did.

"Portions of my CD sales go into a fund. I and many of my colleagues hope to open a school based on talent, financed by the artists who've made it instead of the ones *trying* to make it."

"Admirable." Therin leaned back in his chair. His smirk held tinges of regret though. "I wish it were so easy to get a group of politicians on the same page like that."

The two would have delved back into the rest of their meals to further conversation. The laughter and easy mood, however, was interrupted when Vaughn Burgess approached the table.

"Accept my apologies…please." Momentarily taken aback by Therin's breakfast partner, Vaughn was undoubtedly captivated.

"Kianti Lawrence, my right arm, Vaughn Burgess." Therin enjoyed the man's mesmerized expression.

Vaughn, in fact, seemed to have forgotten all about Therin's presence. He leaned close to take Kianti's hand. "I enjoyed your playing very much," he told her.

Kianti bowed her head graciously. "I appreciate you saying that. I thought I may have sounded a bit rushed last night."

"Nonsense." Vaughn's entranced expression turned woeful. "I do apologize for the interruption. I'm gonna have to steal this guy." He glanced toward Therin before smiling again at Kianti and stepping back to offer the couple privacy.

Therin took her hand next. "This was nice."

She nodded. "Yes."

"This must be important or else he wouldn't be here. Always on my back for not relaxing more." Therin spoke the last sentence a bit louder for Vaughn's benefit.

Kianti bit her lip playfully to stifle her laughter. "It's okay. I understand, really."

"When do you leave?" he asked.

"This afternoon."

He let her see his frown. "I'll see you before you leave."

She placed her hand across his. "Handle your business."

"I promise," he said, giving her hand a squeeze and standing as the waiter returned. "This is on me." He tossed several bills to the table and pushed several more into the young man's hand.

Kianti's eyes followed Therin until he was gone from the dining room.

"This had better be damned good," Therin growled to Vaughn as they rounded the corner.

Vaughn's voice was uncharacteristically hollow. "It's not. It's not good at all."

The weight which had lifted from Therin's shoulders during the time spent with Kianti fell like an anvil when he and Vaughn returned to the suite. The conversation he'd escaped from earlier, and hoped would be over by the time he returned, seemed to have taken on new life. It wasn't long before he discovered why.

"Dammit," Therin growled upon viewing the file on one of his staff assistants, Ruby Loro.

Absolute silence settled in the suite for the first time that morning.

Therin Rucker's calm demeanor was a constant that his staff respected and thrived in the midst of. Though he often preferred to step back and do more observing,

Therin encouraged discussion and debate. He felt they were the greatest tools in running effective campaigns and encouraging loyalty. Witnessing a loss of temper from someone so focused and deliberate was as fascinating as it was disconcerting.

"This is bullshit." Therin's voice was a little more than a whisper. He massaged the back of his neck and slanted Vaughn a dark look.

"Agreed." Vaughn raised his hands defensively. "But it's still gonna have to be dealt with…on several levels."

"I should talk to her." Therin rifled through the file. "Has she seen this mess?"

"No, um…it was uh—stuck inside your complimentary copy of this morning's *USA TODAY*," Morgan Felts explained.

Therin began a pace of the suite's living area. "Anybody contact the office to confirm that?"

"Ther, nobody's heard a damn thing," Gary Bryce chimed in.

Peter Stanson used the pen he held to gesture toward the file. "I think it's safe to say that whoever left that crap meant for you to see it first and to decide how best to keep it quiet."

"By keeping my damn mouth shut," Therin guessed, walking past the table and swiping a stack of papers to the floor.

Vaughn took advantage of the clean area of the table and helped himself to a seat. "I don't think it's as much about keeping your mouth shut as it is about using it to promote other interests."

"Screw that." Therin's voice was monotone.

The other four men in the room exchanged looks.

They'd known Therin long enough to know that the flat tone of his voice signified his mood shifting into dark territory.

"Would it really be that much of an issue to throw a little chatter toward your other endeavors?" Peter asked.

Therin turned, pushing hands into the deep pockets of his sweats.

"The pockets you open…there's enough to go around, right?" The look Peter received then had him swallowing uncomfortably while lifting his hands in submission.

Vaughn reached for the file and perused the lurid film shots. The webpage printouts showed covers of adult DVDs featuring Ruby Loro when she'd come to the U.S. illegally and willing to do anything to stay there.

"We suspected all along that these folks you're rattling were sons of bitches. All of our research into what few leads we have proves their allegiance is to the manufacture of the weapons and military strength over the education of the nation's kids," Vaughn said while shaking his head at the damaging items inside the file. "What they've just done proves they're willing to go to any lengths to draw you over to their side but this…" he groaned. "She's a sweetheart, Ther. She doesn't deserve to have this tossed up in her face. She's not this woman anymore."

"Hell, you don't think I know that, V?" Therin's mood had journeyed into an even darker abyss. "Get her on the phone, G."

"What are you gonna do?" Peter asked, while Gary made the call.

Therin's expression was unreadable. "I'll know that when I talk to her."

Chapter 3

Kianti's shoulders slumped when she returned to her suite and found it filled with her travel companions. They each turned to fix her with unfriendly looks when she strolled into the room.

Cube even ceased his raid on the snack safe. "Well, well, look who decided to show up and let us know she wasn't somewhere havin' a heart attack!"

Winton was on the phone and only remarked with a slow shake of his head to illustrate his irritation. "Yeah…yeah we should be in by six," he continued.

"Mmm-hmm." Khan didn't look up while he surfed channels. "No note or nothin'. Your *cook* wasn't sure whether to start breakfast." His slanted stare narrowed further when he and Cube dissolved into laughter over the dig at Brody.

Dr. Brody Parker simply leaned against the doorway to the bedroom, arms folded across his chest.

"Can't I even eat breakfast on my own?" Kianti tossed aside her black tote.

"Ah, breakfast." Brody pushed off the doorway. "You mean that stuff we practically have to force you to eat?"

"Can't a person improve their eating habits?"

"Of course, but this is *you* we're talkin' about," Brody countered.

Kianti threw up her hands. "I don't want to waste time going back and forth over this."

"Oh, we know that." Khan chuckled. "Obviously you prefer spending your time with the ambassador."

"Hmph." She folded her arms over her sweater. "And did your spies tell you I was at the table long before he got there?"

"Maybe y'all planned it that way last night," Cube chided with a sly wink and a mouthful of Skittles.

"Did you take your pill?"

"Yes!" Kianti snapped at Brody's question.

"That's funny since, according to my count it doesn't look like you've taken one in over two weeks."

Kianti stilled but for a moment. "You went through my stuff?" She exploded, her dark gaze more brilliant in the wake of anger.

Feathers unruffled, Brody merely shrugged. "Are you trying to kill yourself?"

"Yes. Yes, Brody, that's exactly what I'm trying to do. Didn't you see the coffin catalog on the nightstand when you were going through my things?"

The room quieted. Winton had finished his call. Khan shut off the television. The group had had their run-ins regarding Kianti's outlook toward her health, but never had she gone so far as to shun the pills which kept her heart rate stable. The sudden spikes in pulse had plagued Kianti since childhood.

She hid her face in her hands and inhaled deeply for a moment. "Guys…I'm trying to live. I don't want to be tied to those things my entire life."

"Those *things* help keep you alive."

She smiled over Brody's soft reminder. "And I stopped taking them four weeks ago." She studied the surprise in his dark eyes. "Guess you didn't bother to check my previous bottle."

"Dammit, Key!" Khan threw the remote to the coffee table. "Hell, that's just stupid!"

"And I don't expect any of you to understand." She pointed a finger toward the floor. "You don't know what it's like not being able to do what you love without some crutch—not to be able to have someone to love for fear of…"

The guys exchanged meaningful looks over the top of Kianti's head. Slowly, they crowded her. Cube was first to draw her close and kiss the top of her head.

Brody squeezed her arms. "Don't you know they'd have to bury us, too, if anything ever happened to you?"

"You're our meal ticket, girl." Cube shook her gently. "Not to mention our pass to all the best parties."

Soft laughter rose among the five. Brody and Kianti had known each other since childhood. Kianti met Cube, Khan and Winton in college where she'd tutored Winton in English Lit while he'd tutored her in Advanced Calculus. Cube, Khan and Winton shared a dorm suite with Brody. Despite the unorthodox dynamic, the group had developed a close-knit relationship that bordered on familial.

Kianti knocked her fist against the denim shirt covering Cube's wide chest. "Guys, I've been off the pills for four weeks. Can't we just wait and see what happens?"

As a response, Kianti heard all sorts of curses and other low sounds of disapproval.

"Hell, Brody's the doctor." Winton rubbed his fingers across the faded haircut he sported. "I have to agree with Khan though, this is plain stupid." He tugged Kianti out of Cube's embrace and into his own. "We hear what you're sayin', babe, but this is only one pill. Some folks have to take ten times as much medication."

"And people overcome their need for medication every day." She tugged the zipper dangling from his windbreaker. "Like you said, some people take ten times as much as I do."

Bested, Winton waved his hand and turned Kianti toward Brody. "*You* talk to her."

"All right, Key, we'll do it your way." The doctor stunned everyone, including his patient. "But understand—" he wagged a finger "—you're backing me— all of us—into a corner here. We can't force you to do a damn thing when it comes right down to it. This is your life, but you've put us in charge of protecting it. Look for us to be even more aggressive in keeping you safe, calm and rested. Even if we have to tie you down in a bed to make it happen."

Khan nudged her side. "That part'll be easy since we've all thought of doing it at one time or another." He winked, waiting for the smile he was trying to rouse from her. He succeeded, joining in when she grinned.

"If none of this works, you're back on the pills.

Agreed?" Brody brought the seriousness back to the moment.

Kianti's nod came slowly but with a great deal of relief. She no longer had to hide.

"All right, y'all, we should go," Brody told the guys and squeezed Kianti's hand. "You rest up. We're out of here in a few hours."

"Are they around her all the time?"

"Pretty much from what I gather."

"Well, who are they? To her, I mean?"

Therin began questioning Vaughn about Kianti Lawrence shortly after the rest of the staff left them alone in the living area.

"She's not…*involved* with them all, is she?" Therin smiled, knowing the idea was ludicrous. Still, for a woman like that…it wouldn't be a difficult thing to keep a man *or four* dangling.

"It's not like that, man," Vaughn said through his chuckling.

"From what you gather?" Therin countered, watching as Vaughn shrugged.

"What's got you so interested here?"

Therin's expression was incredulous. "Did you take a good look at her this morning?"

"Damn straight I did." Vaughn swore while raising his hands for confirmation. "She's a goddess but she doesn't live in this hotel. Neither do you. You don't even live in the country—technically."

Therin had moved over to the windows and sat on the back of the oversize chair facing them.

Vaughn followed. "Talk to me, T. What is it about this one?"

"Hell, man, what's the big deal?" His grin was forced. "I only asked if she's attached to her bodyguards."

"Simple as that, huh?" Vaughn rubbed at the receding edge of his hairline. His handsome honey-toned face was a picture of disbelief. "How many times did you zone out this morning, man?"

"Understandable." Therin tapped his hand to the front of the sweatshirt he wore. "I wasn't particularly interested in the conversation when I walked out of here earlier."

"Mmm-hmm, and you weren't all too pleased that I interrupted your breakfast to ask you to join us back up here."

"Like I said, just didn't want to be part of the discussion."

"What do you expect could come of this, T? All right, all right," he said when Therin flashed him a cold look. "May I at least ask if you're trying to make sure you're not playing with someone else's toy?"

Therin smiled then. "No. I only want to know whose toy I'm about to take away."

Vaughn burst into laughter and nodded when his boss asked that he check out Kianti Lawrence and her crew.

Kianti bit her lip and tried to cast covert glances around the lobby. She and the guys would be leaving for the airport as soon as the car was packed. Therin had promised to say goodbye.

She bowed her head, snuggling into the high collar of the black cashmere coat she wore. *Idiot,* she chastised herself. That brief acquaintance was over and done with. What else could it have been?

Distance wasn't the only deciding factor there, either. She was sick of involvements that dissolved because of a weak heart. She smiled unamused and wondered what had done more damage to her heart—her illness or the amount of times her heart had been broken. She felt hands squeeze her arms and masked her disappointment when she saw Winton at her side.

"We're all set. You got everything?"

Kianti risked another glance around the spacious lobby and then nodded. "Let's go home," she said.

"Ruby? Ruby, calm down. For the third time, I didn't call to fire you."

"Sorry, Therin. Sorry," Ruby Loro blubbered, sniffled and gasped over the phone. "I shouldn't have done it—keeping my past a secret like that. I just—just felt like I didn't have a choice. Stupid!" she called herself and hiccupped on a few more sobs. "I thought...the movies were the easiest choice—quickest path to success, or so I thought. God..." she moaned and broke into another stretch of tears. "I'm sorry..."

"Ruby. Calm yourself." Therin's voice was patience personified.

"I'll resign." Ruby hiccupped the words. "I'll resign my post. The last thing I want is to cast a shadow over all the good you're doing."

"And you know me well enough to know I don't want a resignation any more than I want to fire you." Leaning forward on the sofa, Therin braced elbows to his knees. "What I want is for you to think. Did anyone approach you about this? Who knew Ruby Loro was once Spanish Heat?"

"Jesus," Ruby hissed at the sound of the name she'd filmed under. "No one knew my real name. Not even the movie people." She laughed shortly. "They really didn't care about background checks, or whether I knew English for that matter. Knowing lines wasn't a big issue, you see?"

"Right…" His hand flexed around the slim cordless. "I'm sorry, Ruby, for making you remember this crap."

"I don't have any family or friends except for the ones I've made while living and working in Canada."

"Does that mean you could handle this coming out?" Silence met Therin's question. "I don't intend on bending over for these fools."

"And I'm tired of hiding. You can rip them a new one for all I care."

"Don't you have vacation time you've been hoarding?"

"Almost a month," Ruby boasted.

"Take it and longer if you need it." Therin left the sofa and went to look out over the Spokane view. "I'm about to call the bluff on these jackasses. I don't need you caught up in it yet if it's not necessary."

"Thank you, Therin. Thanks for believing in me. Most…" She sniffled lightly. "Most would have judged and not given another thought to firing me."

"Well, I happen to know, like and respect Ruby Loro too much to lose her." He turned his back on the view then. "You get lost and I'll be in touch when the coast is halfway clear."

"Right. Oh! Therin? You had a call come in from a Shepard Yale. Is he—?"

"Yeah…one and the same." Therin confirmed Ruby's suspicions on the caller's identity while wondering what the retired general wanted with him. He didn't realize he'd spoken aloud.

"The general was a military liaison toward the end of his career. He smoothed more ruffled feathers and thwarted more potential uprisings than anyone who held the post before or since." Ruby sighed after giving the rundown. "Maybe something's about to go down and he wants to consult with you."

"Maybe…" Therin tapped his cleft chin and considered the words briefly before turning his focus back to Ruby. "You go pack. We'll talk soon, all right?"

"All right, and Therin? Thanks."

Vaughn came to the living area just as the call ended. "How'd she take it?"

"Not well."

Vaughn nodded. "Did she have any idea who could've leaked this about her past?"

Therin tossed the phone to the sofa. "Not one. Folks she knew back then weren't really interested in her past, but what she could do for 'em in front of the camera, you know?"

"Right…" Vaughn's mouth tightened.

"Ruby said a call came in from Shep Yale."

"The general?" Vaughn dropped to the sofa and listened as Therin shared Ruby's idea about the man wanting a consult on something about to pop off. "Could be," he agreed, realizing the only way to know anything for sure would be to meet with the revered general.

"Hell, V, the man's been retired for how long?"

"And someone with that kind of power never fully retires. Those connections, all that knowledge—it's always relevant."

Silence fell while the two contemplated. Suddenly, Therin's curse was filling the room.

Kianti flashed through his mind. "What's the time?" he asked even as he checked the Swiss timepiece around his wrist. "Hell…"

"What?" Vaughn stood.

Therin was already halfway out the door.

"I'm so sorry, Mr. Ambassador." Nenda Watts apologized for the third time since Therin arrived at the front desk. She'd just told him he'd missed Kianti, who had left for the airport ten minutes earlier with her entourage.

"Shit." Therin brought a fist down to the glossy maple front desk while grinding the muscle in his jaw. Turning slowly, he stared absently past the windows lining the bright, elegantly designed hotel lobby.

Was it worth it? he asked himself, wondering if he should chalk up the *chance encounter* as a brief interlude in the chaos that was his life. After all, what could come from an involvement between a busy pianist and a controversial ex-ambassador?

He smiled at the combination. It was a mix best left alone. Smirking then, he turned back to the front desk.

"Where was Ms. Lawrence's flight headed?"

Chapter 4

Pacifica, California

Scottie's Supper Club prided its location for the bulk of its success. With a view to marvel over, the jazz establishment catered to patrons practically round the clock. Visitors to the club could enjoy a spectacular day or evening view and music from some of the most noted performers in the country.

Kianti had the pleasure of enjoying the club as a patron as well as a performer. She often dropped in to surprise Scott Sanders with an impromptu jam session with his in-house band, led by vocalist Eli Waverly and drummer Shelton Innes. Still, the fact that Scottie's was located less than ten minutes from her home, was Kianti's favorite thing about the club.

Having a close friendship with the drummer was a plus as well. Shelton Innes recognized her as part of the audience one evening shortly after Kianti had started attending the group's performances several years earlier. He kept the spotlight on her until she had accepted his offer to join them on stage. The set was one of her fondest memories, and she and Shelton had been the best of friends ever since. It was Shelton who pulled Kianti onboard in the collaboration for the school that several other musicians hoped to open for musically gifted kids.

Kianti often made a point of stopping in to chat with the group after she'd been out of town performing. She waited a few nights to make an appearance there following her return from Washington. She'd come prepared to perform and the group didn't hesitate to demand her presence on stage shortly after she arrived at Scottie's that evening.

The group was in the midst of a mellow albeit affecting session when Therin arrived at the club. It wasn't hard finding her address. He'd arrived only to find her on her way out. Thankfully, it hadn't been too difficult to follow her to the club that was only a short distance away. Now what? he asked himself while claiming a seat at the bar in hopes of keeping himself somewhat shielded from her line of sight. He took a seat near the end of the bar figuring Kianti wouldn't notice him there. He wondered whether she'd even notice him at all. They really hadn't had all that much time together. Thinking on that, he couldn't ignore the question that had been plaguing him since he headed south instead of north to Canada upon leaving Washington State. Exactly what was he doing there?

He decided it was best not to seek an answer on that

yet. Therin only knew that Kianti Lawrence had him curious and he wanted to find out more.

Bringing fist to chin, he settled in to observe her behind the glossy black piano. The animated look on her rich cinnamon-toned face, as she talked with the members of the group, brought a smile to Therin's face. No doubt she was a lovely thing to look at. He wondered how much of that played into her success, though no one could argue against her talent.

Therin recalled their breakfast conversation then and the relaxing mood he'd sensed surrounding her. He remembered the feel of her small foot when he'd held it and grinned on the memory. He'd never enjoyed breakfast or a conversation more.

The set was nearing its end, tugging Therin from his reverie as he once again observed her with the band— especially the drummer. It was clear that they were close, which had him smiling but not in a completely amused way. He thought back to her entourage—the four men who'd given him the distinct impression that they'd lay down their lives for her. How could they not feel that way? he queried silently as the muscle twitched along his jawbone when her drummer friend pulled her in for a hug.

Get the hell out of here, Therin, he warned himself. He should go before she had any idea he was near. An involvement like this would never work. He lived in Canada, for Pete's sake! Watching her near the stage and chatting away, Therin's grim expression vanished and a smile emerged.

"Could I bring you anything, sir?"

Therin looked up at the young woman who'd approached the table. She held a pen poised over the small round tray she carried.

"I'd like to have a drink sent over to the pianist." He nodded slowly toward the stage.

The waitress smiled while jotting down the instruction. "Shall I tell Ms. Lawrence who's being so generous?"

"I'll remain anonymous." Therin's bright gaze was still focused on Kianti.

"Not a problem." The waitress cast one last lingering and blatantly flattering gaze at her mysterious customer.

Therin stood and dropped a few bills to the woman's tray and then graced her with a sly wink before turning to make his way out of the club.

Dammit, Key, get over it!

Kianti smacked the soapy loofah pad against her thigh while issuing herself the order. She was acting like some love-struck girl whose family was moving away and taking her from a boy she'd known all of two seconds. Granted, she'd known the sexy ex-ambassador for a little longer. Still, nothing had happened that meant anything meaningful or otherwise would come from it.

Otherwise. She let the word linger in her head and felt a heat that had nothing to do with the shower spray hitting her skin. She would have enjoyed experiencing *otherwise* with Therin Rucker.

She smacked herself again with the loofah pad. All that would have gotten her was a trip to the hospital. If her heart struggled to withstand exertion from a piano performance, how would it withstand a sexual encounter?

Smirking then, she told herself that it might *withstand* just fine. Therin Rucker came across as quite the gentleman. If that persona carried over into the bedroom, perhaps there wouldn't be much exertion required.

Kianti applied more gel to the pad and considered the idea. Something told her the dashing politician left his manners at the door when pleasure was at stake. She sensed a fire, something unrelenting at rest beneath that polished exterior. Yes, there was a side to the man that, if unleashed sexually, could require much…exertion on the part of its recipient.

She pressed a hand to her belly and moaned. She'd gone so long without indulging in that very enjoyable pastime. Only to herself would she admit that given another couple of days in Therin Rucker's presence, she would've had him in her bed and *exerting* herself to the fullest.

The loofah smacked her thigh a third time. "Get over it," she growled.

Somewhere a phone rang. Kianti leaned out of the shower to grab the wall mount next to the stall.

"Ms. Lawrence…Casey O'Dell down here at the gate. You've got a guest here. Mr. Therin Rucker."

Her hand returned to her belly and then to her mouth where she tapped her fingers to her lips.

"Ms. Lawrence?"

Kianti took stock of her appearance in the mirror across from the shower. "Send him up."

* * *

Therin inhaled the second he stepped from the elevator that deposited him in the middle of a room that whispered serenity and expansive comfort. Softly lit, the living room's mellow appeal was evident not only by the cream-on-gold furnishings but also by the long window overlooking the ocean from the home's rocky perch. He smiled then, further eased by the sound of her voice.

"Mr. Ambassador."

Therin turned and any ease he was experiencing was quickly replaced by need. Somewhere—somehow he was able to latch on to restraint.

"I'm sorry..." He bowed his head while uttering the apology. "I, um... Your guard didn't tell me you..."

Kianti tossed back her head. "It's okay. I told him to send you on up."

"I promised to say goodbye." He spouted the first thing that came to his mind.

She bit her lip on a smile. "Well, I hope you're not about to do *that*."

Therin rolled his eyes. *To hell with it.* It'd serve her right for greeting him in a towel with that gorgeous mane of hair piled atop her head and bubbles still clinging to her cinnamon skin. With that in mind, he bounded over, snagged the front of the towel and drew her close.

Kianti was an eager and immediate participant in the thorough kiss. Her moans raised an instant after his tongue began its enthusiastic duel with hers. Wavering and shamefully erotic, the sounds came from the back of her throat. She stood on her toes and her fingers curled tight into the tails of the burgundy shirt hanging outside the black carpenter's jeans he wore.

Therin needed to cast off the heat about to consume him but he was already caressing the seductive swells of her breasts. His sleek ebony brows drew closer and he deepened the kiss. Any second, and her towel would be on the floor.

He pulled away then. "You need to get dressed." His tone was gruff and he turned away. One of them had to exercise a cool head. Why? He had no idea, but the thought had managed to give him pause regardless.

"I didn't ask you to stop," she sweetly reminded him.

"Unfortunately," he winced and realized he'd spoken aloud, before massaging the bridge of his nose. "Get dressed." His tone was almost pleading then. While he intended to have her—*all* of her—it was far too soon to indulge in the many things he wanted to do with her. "Kianti…"

She waved toward the living room. "Have a seat, I'll be right back." She watched him stroll toward the window instead. *Yes, manners left at the door when pleasure was at stake,* she silently confirmed on her way out of the room.

"Is this better?" she asked minutes later.

Therin tried not to stare. Her gray lounge dress had its wrist-hugging sleeves and was made of a clingy cotton material. While covering every inch of her skin, it emphasized every dip and curve she possessed. The only thing on his mind then, was whether or not she was nude beneath it.

He waited on her to choose a seat. Kianti noted that

he seemed pleased that she didn't select the sofa but curled up on one of the overstuffed chairs flanking it.

"May I get you anything?" she asked once he'd settled on the chair before her.

"I'm good." His light, deep-set eyes scanned the room in one continuous take. "Some place you've got here."

"Isn't it?" She propped a fist against her thick hair trussed up in a flouncy ponytail and smiled. "Got it from an elderly scientist I met after a concert. The lower level where you came in used to be his lab. I converted it into a private studio."

"Impressive."

"Very. That elevator was once the only access—comes right up through the cliffs the house sits on."

Therin whistled.

Kianti shrugged. "The guys forbid me to take it. But if it gets stuck, the top panels open and there's a ladder that leads up to the house."

"Good to know." He laughed.

"They had me have the top-level access constructed." She smoothed her hands over the dress's long snug sleeves. "If you'd come past the other houses, I could've greeted you personally."

"Or not—considering you were in the um…shower." He cleared his throat over the last word.

Kianti shifted on the chair. "You must've just missed us when we left the other day," she added quickly to change the subject. "Not to mention I wasn't expecting you." She gave Therin a slight wink.

"Yeah." A quick frown marred the sensual elegance of his features. "There was business."

"Not good business?" She tilted her head inquisitively.

"Is there such a thing?" He shook his head and rubbed his hands together. "I only wanted you to know that I hadn't broken my promise."

"And I appreciate you coming all this way to tell me that." Her dark eyes twinkled knowingly.

He braced his elbows to his knees. "I did have an ulterior motive."

"Shall I guess?"

Therin's thoughts returned to the kiss. "You, uh... You know about my involvement with EYES?" he asked, figuring that line of discussion was safest. At her nod, he continued. "I'm hoping to organize an event—a weekend thing. I already have a host of performers lined up, but when I heard you play, I knew I had to have you."

Both pairs of eyes faltered on the suggestive tone of the last few words. Therin focused on the bridge he made with his fingers while Kianti shifted once more in her chair.

"I'd be honored," she said, smiling when he looked up. "We'll have to talk about the time—schedules, locations and such...."

"You'll probably need to spend time in Vancouver—to practice at my place there. Get a feel for the venue... The piano's top-of-the-line but I don't profess to be a musician, so—" he smirked "—I'll leave things like tuning and pitch up to the professionals."

"I'll check my schedule and we can go from there."

"Sounds good." His gaze narrowed toward the

window. "I didn't mean to disturb you so late in the day. Have you eaten?"

She pulled her legs out from beneath her and scooted toward the edge of the chair. "I was about to put something on. I'd love it if you stayed."

Again, the kiss resumed its place at the front of his thoughts. Therin knew a lengthier stay might not be the best idea.

"I shouldn't intrude on your night," he said.

Kianti shrugged and toyed with a lock of her hair. "I usually spend the first few days after a performance holed up here just to get my bearings."

"Is that something you usually do alone?" Therin averted his gaze as his voice dipped into a softer octave.

"Yeah…usually… Why?" She caught the smile he gave at her response.

He leaned back and propped an elbow to each arm of the chair. "Your…entourage. It's hard to believe not one of them has made a play for you."

"Hmph." Kianti grinned as though the summation wasn't a surprise to her. "Few people understand our dynamic. They nod and smile when I say we're like family but no one really believes it." She smiled off into the distance. "We do tease each other relentlessly but we trust each other, love each other, stick up for and bully one another when we feel it's necessary. But they've got their *own* love lives."

"And you?" His bright stare was probing then, daring her to look away. "You expect me to believe your work is all you need?"

"No." She shook her head slowly yet decisively. "There've been involvements." She flopped back on the chair. "Any Google search could've told you that. But nothing has gone on in that area for years now. So…" Her tone sounded more refreshing then. "No need to worry over being a home wrecker, Mr. Ambassador. Will you stay? I'm a pretty decent cook."

He smiled. "What's for dinner?"

Vancouver, BC, Canada~

"The old man won't breathe a word about it," Morgan Felts snapped when he slammed down his office phone.

"Is there anybody on his staff who might know why he wants to talk to Therin?" Peter Stanson asked.

"The general's retired," Vaughn reminded them while he sat on the edge of Morgan's desk and tossed a wad of paper back and forth. "Most of his staff is back in D.C. on other assignments."

Gary Bryce turned from the coffee tray. "Could still be worth checking out," he said. "See if he made remarks about anything before he left his post."

"Has Therin ever met with the general before?" Peter watched the other men shake their heads in response to his question.

Morgan threw a pen across his desk. "This is weird— an uncomfortable weird. Guess we're stuck waiting 'til Therin gets back. Where the hell is he, anyway?"

"Being real tight-lipped about it." Vaughn shrugged beneath the crisp baby blue of his shirt. "Said he'd be back in a few days."

"Gary, man, maybe if you checked out the general's former staff, somethin' might turn up." Peter tugged at his earlobe and looked doubtful.

"We could be wasting our time," Vaughn warned.

"Maybe, but we need to be a step ahead on everything from here on out. Especially after what happened with Ruby."

Gary agreed with Peter's assessment and raised his coffee mug in mock toast. "I'm on it," he said on his way out of the office.

"Say, Vaughn," Peter called while they shuffled from Morgan's office. "What's up with Ther, seriously?"

Vaughn clapped Peter's back. "For a change, the guy has got something other than politics on his mind."

"Who ever said musicians aren't paid well?" Therin asked as he and Kianti rounded out their after-dinner tour of her home. It went without saying that he was very impressed.

"Well, Dr. Chapin and his wife really loved my music." Kianti smoothed her hands up and down her arms as memories resurfaced. "They came to all the shows I had in the area back when I was just starting out." She stopped to lean against the railing along the walkway where they strolled.

"Later, I found out they had all my CDs—even the little promotional ones I put out when I was trying to get noticed." Her dark eyes held a poignant gleam as she stared out at the Pacific crashing against the rocks below. "They left me the house. His foundation got all the scientific equipment and the youth home they supported got all the furnishings."

"Nice." Therin appreciated the artwork lining the wall along the walkway. "Very nice," he added when they entered the studio.

"I do most of my practicing here. It's one of the few places where I don't feel pressured."

Therin watched her fingers graze the glossy top of the baby grand piano. "You're lucky. There aren't even a *few* places I could claim."

"Must be nice to be needed."

"It's been nicer."

Kianti leaned against the piano. "Do I sense another career change?" She braced her elbows back on the baby grand and regarded him with playful suspicion. "Just exactly what *do* you do for a living?"

He chuckled, smoothing a hand down a sideburn. "Guess I do whatever I damn well please. But I *choose* to torture myself for a worthy cause. Basically, I connect people with similar interests."

"Interests here being educational."

He nodded. "I know a lot of philanthropists who not only like giving money to various endeavors but appreciate knowing about others who share their interests in those endeavors." He shrugged and strolled around the piano. "My family and my work put me in contact with many of them. I spend a lot of time bringing them together for worthy causes." He frowned, not wanting to speak much about work when he was with her.

The feeling of serenity he'd experienced backstage with her after the concert, and again the next morning, had returned. He only wanted to savor the moment and cast out all the rest.

"May I make a request?" He motioned toward the piano.

Kianti's grin sparked the faint dimple she possessed.

"Your request, sir?" she asked once she'd rounded the Baby Grand and claimed her place.

"Do you know 'Skating'?"

Her laughter filled the room at his mention of the *Peanuts* tune by the Vince Guaraldi Trio. "Take a seat." She waved in the direction of the navy-and-tan living set across the room.

The performance began. Therin was, of course, captivated, mesmerized by the eloquence with which she played. Gradually, his attention turned from the playing to the woman. Instead of relaxing in the living area, he propped an elbow to the top of the piano and watched her. Her body was tiny albeit curvaceous beneath the lounge dress, which hadn't ceased driving him out of his mind since she'd returned to the living room wearing it.

He enjoyed the look of her coarse hair piled in a high ponytail. The locks bounced about her lovely face like a storm cloud.

"Is that what you had in mind?" Kianti asked once the piece had ended.

"Almost," he said and leaned down for a kiss.

She whimpered before his mouth even touched hers. She clenched her hands, praying for the will not to grab him for fear that he might back away. She let him command the kiss, giving in more eagerly as she stood and he drew her flush against him.

A low sigh of male satisfaction left his throat when Therin straightened and drew Kianti snug against his chest. Resting against the side of the piano, he deepened the kiss thrusting his tongue slowly yet unrelentingly.

Kianti's hands kneaded his forearms and biceps to

test the strength at rest there beneath the dark fabric of his shirt. She moaned in the midst of suckling his tongue. Arching closer and rubbing herself against him in shameless abandon, she cursed the dress covering her skin.

Back off... Therin told himself, but chose to set aside the order for a few seconds. He wanted longer to indulge in just a bit more of her. The serenity she radiated took on a more potent aura during their second kiss. He had no will or intention to stop it.

Somehow though, he did resist—a feat in itself considering her moans told him not to stop. Her voice was soft, helpless yet deliberate. The tone sent the strength right from his legs causing him to lean more fully into the piano.

Kianti shuddered and snuggled deeper into the embrace as she assumed a more controlling role in the duel being fought between their tongues. She gripped his shirt as though it were her lifeline while inhaling the appealing scent of his cologne. There was that familiar voice in her head still singing its same old song. It told her to end this, but how could she when *this* was so sweet and so dearly missed....

Therin set her away suddenly and blinked. That familiar voice in his head reminded him of their distance and the demands of their lives. How could they work?

"I really need to go," he said, keeping his hands firm at her elbows to keep her and him at bay. "Thank you for dinner."

"Will I see you again?"

He kissed her forehead and let his mouth linger there. "I'll be at your door for breakfast."

"If you stay, you could wake up to breakfast."

"Kianti…" he pressed his forehead to hers. "You're killin' me." He kissed her cheek. "Good night."

Chapter 5

Brody's handsome face registered frustration when he arrived at Kianti's early the next morning and smelled breakfast in the air. When he asked what they were having and was told he wasn't invited, the disappointment emerged.

Kianti was in full gear when her doctor arrived to check in on her. She'd totally forgotten about the house call and hoped he'd be gone by the time Therin arrived. Tossing the dish towel she held to the counter, she promptly thrust out her wrist for him to check her pulse.

Brody saw to his duty, though his dark gaze gradually narrowed and he took a closer look around the airy lavender and white kitchen. "Am I interrupting anything?"

"Not yet," she sang.

"This is good," he said in reference to her pulse, but squeezed her wrist. "For now," he added.

Kianti rolled her eyes. "Don't start."

"What do you think you're doing?" He took a seat at one of the stools near the breakfast nook. "And don't bother acting like you don't know what or *who* I'm talking about."

"Brody, please." She stalked back to the stove and made a pretense of checking the eggs in the warmer. "I'm about to have breakfast with an incredible man and...see where things go from there."

"And the direction you're hoping for is the bedroom."

She slammed her hand to the counter and turned. "Damn you." Her temper peaked when she felt the pressure of tears.

"Damn," he hissed when she rushed from the kitchen. Leaving the stool, he caught her before she cleared the doorway. "I'm sorry." He pressed both hands to his chest in a show of sincerity. "The last thing I want is to upset you."

"Oh, that I believe, since feeling upset is a lively emotion. Feeling alive is the last thing any of you want me to experience."

"Do you really believe that?" His voice was hushed.

"Prove it, then. Let me have this—don't interfere."

"Key—"

"You promised you'd back off."

Brody smoothed a hand across his low-cut Afro. "That promise was in reference to the pills."

"Hmph." Kianti shoved both hands into the back pockets of her snug capris and began a slow pace of the kitchen.

"Pout all you want, but we plan to be focused in hard and heavy on every other aspect of your life."

"Stay out of this Brody—that goes for you and your cronies. There isn't even anything going on. The man lives in Vancouver, for Heaven's sake!"

"All right. All right." Brody bowed his head and decided to give it a rest. He walked over to kiss her cheek and turned her toward the stove. "Your bacon's done," he said, before leaving.

Kianti watched him pull keys from his khakis and go. Then she went to handle the bacon. Brody's cautions returned though. Exactly what *did* she think she was doing? She'd done a fine job of ignoring the question, which had made a nice little camp in the back of her mind.

She thought back to her behavior when Therin visited the day before. She'd never been shy with men. She believed in being up front about what she wanted, as opposed to playing coy games to go after it.

Where Therin Rucker was concerned, God, she wanted him. Perhaps that was simply because her sex life was so lacking. Perhaps it was because he was so very appealing.

Perhaps she wanted to test how ready she was to live life to its fullest without the aid of her trusty meds. And what if she wasn't ready? A relationship—hell. *Any* sort of involvement with the very sexy ex-ambassador or anyone else, for that matter, would be out of the question.

Then there was her playing—her passion. Was she really ready to risk that by unchaining herself from those pills?

And what of Therin himself? Didn't he deserve to know of her condition? Kianti shook her head and began wiping down the already spotless countertop. She didn't need to think of that just then. *Perhaps* she wasn't as ready to live this part of her life as she thought.

Therin whistled a soft tune and was grabbing his keys from the message table when his phone vibrated next to them. He grumbled low, spotting Vaughn's name on the faceplate. Silently, he debated on whether or not to reply. Last thing he wanted was more drama filtering into his time with Kianti.

"Yeah, V?" He answered anyway, while checking his watch.

"Hey…you talk to the general yet?"

"Mmm, the general…that's a no."

"Why not?" Vaughn laughed shortly.

Therin settled partially on the desk. "Other things on my mind."

"Ah…the lovely and gifted Kianti Lawrence." Vaughn's laughter was easier then. "Look, man, you know I approve of you takin' time out to enjoy yourself but have you thought about how complicated this could be?"

Therin wouldn't admit that was almost all he could think about. Those thoughts, however, were easy to cast off when he recalled how alive he felt when he was with her. He wasn't ready to let go of that yet and honestly didn't know when he would be.

"Ther?"

"Did you check out her entourage?"

Vaughn cleared his throat. "Yeah, um— They, um,

they're almost like a family. They don't share blood but they share history. All met up during their college years. Kianti divided her time between a hellacious practice schedule mixed with her music curriculum. She and Parker—Brody—go back the furthest. They grew up together."

Therin frowned over that discovery but didn't take long to mull it over.

"Therin… Did Kianti talk about Parker's role in her crew?"

Therin stroked his jaw absently and tried to remember. "She said he was her cook. Why?"

"Because Brody Parker has a medical degree."

Therin's hand paused on his jaw. "Medicine?"

"Cardiology is his specialty."

"You're sure?"

"I *double*-checked to make sure."

Therin's light stare traveled the hotel room in an absent manner.

"You think the guy's walkin' around with a med degree but prefers to play cook to a musical genius?" Vaughn pondered.

Therin managed a chuckle. "I doubt it."

"Wonder why she didn't tell you? You want me to dig more? I'm sure I can find—"

"No, no, V. This is good." Therin bumped his fist against the cleft in his chin. "I'll ask when the time is right."

"I take that to mean you plan on getting to know her better?"

"I'll let you know once *I* know, V."

"This may sound corny, but is it fair to say that the

talented Ms. Lawrence is unlike anyone you've ever met?"

Therin's soft smile belied the unexpected pounding in his heart. Just the mention of her name was starting to affect him quite seriously. "It's fair to say it." He finally acknowledged Vaughn's query.

"Can I ask why?"

Therin leaned on the edge of the message table and considered Vaughn's words. "Guess I could be shallow and say it's because she's a sexy dime I want in my bed." He grinned when Vaughn's chuckle came through the line. "And she's definitely that, but there's more to it. I'm gonna need more time to figure out what that means. I wasn't expecting her, V—not one damn bit. All of a sudden, she was just there—right in front of me, and that's where I want her to stay."

Vaughn whistled. "I'm impressed."

"Ha! Good for you. I'm scared," Therin admitted while silently acknowledging that his *fear* was more exciting than terrifying.

"So I guess this means she's more than someone's *toy* you plan on stealing away?"

"She was always more than that. Look, V, let me check in with you later, all right?" Therin added when Vaughn made no further comments.

He waited a beat before leaving the message table, taking a moment to think over the new information he'd received. Did he and Kianti know each other well enough yet for him to ask what role Brody Parker *really* played in her life? How would she react to him prying into that?

Therin thought back to the kiss they'd shared. He

exchanged stroking his jaw for stroking his chest that felt tight with need once those memories began to funnel in. Ending that closeness was the last thing he wanted, but it was way too soon for them to venture down that road.

In light of that, should he even be heading to her place for breakfast? he wondered. He'd barely been able to walk out of there the other day. Clearly, his resistance to her was practically nonexistent. No doubt she'd be just as provocative that morning. Then what would he do? The *right* thing and not take what he wanted from her or take her until neither of them could see straight which was the *only* thing he wanted to do.

Kianti was checking her hair in the dresser mirror and nodded once in approval of the tiny braids that drew her hair back away from her forehead while leaving the rest of the heavy mass draping past her shoulders.

She was turning away from the dresser when the pill bottle caught her eye. Her fist clenched reflexively and she pressed it to her chin before leaning over to grab the bottle. Brushing her thumb across the label as she studied it, she debated on whether to take one just in case....

"Dammit, Key," she said and slammed the bottle back to the dresser. How could she even consider giving up something she was so determined to accomplish in order to indulge in a few moments (hopefully a few hours) with Therin Rucker?

Nothing was worth that. Not even the pleasure he was sure to bring if his kisses were any clue. The bell rang and she inhaled slowly as though resolving the issue in her head.

* * *

"Did you have a horrible time with the traffic?" she asked after greeting Therin at the front door. "It must be a lot different here than it is in Vancouver."

"It wasn't so bad." He shrugged, his light eyes appreciatively taking in her hair and the turquoise halter she wore.

"Why'd you decide to stay there instead of moving back to the States once your post was up?" Kianti asked while heading for the kitchen.

Therin followed, smiling at the fuzzy black slippers that slapped at the glossy hardwoods. "Vancouver's more my style—then there's the place itself. Damn beautiful." His voice softened and at that moment he wasn't referring to the city, but the woman in his line of sight.

"Makes me feel like I'm in a different time—place." He shrugged offering the sudden explanation when she caught him staring. "Keeps me mellow."

Her dark eyes registered understanding. "Is that important to you? To feel mellow?"

"Well…yeah." He smiled on the admission. "I'd say the same is true for you—am I right?"

Kianti didn't hesitate with her nod.

"Is that what your disappearing backstage is about? You make a habit of doing that?" He strolled closer with his thumbs hooked in the belt loops of his denims.

"It helps." She resumed her journey toward the kitchen.

Therin bit his lip on the next question for only a second before deciding to bite the bullet and ask. "Helps with what?"

The long fork she'd reached for hit the cream stovetop with a clatter. "What do you mean?"

"Hell," Therin muttered and took a moment to work his fingers against the muscles tensed at the back of his neck. "I know Brody Parker is a doctor. I thought he might be yours."

She smiled and reached for the fork again. "I assure you, I'm not contagious."

Therin reciprocated the smile. "I didn't suspect that you were." He neared the island and watched her at the stove. "I didn't mean to offend you."

"It's okay." She was already shaking her head. "I definitely can't blame you for asking especially after that pathetic lie I told about Brody being my cook." She laughed shortly over the memory.

Therin took a seat on one of the Chinese stools surrounding the chopping-block-top kitchen island. "Why'd you feel the need to tell me that?"

"Hmph." Kianti turned and leaned against the stove. "Therin, I have a heart condition that can cause a spike in my blood pressure. My playing affects it, as does virtually any overexertion." She toyed with the O-ring at the front of her halter. "I've been taking pills for several years to regulate it. There's no other treatment aside from a heart transplant…maybe." She smirked and blinked to ward off what felt suspiciously like tears.

"If I'd introduced Brody as my doctor that night, I'd have felt obligated to explain all that and…." She grabbed a towel and began to wipe down the counter. "I just didn't want to."

"Why would you feel the need to explain that?" He

rested his arm across the island. "Lots of celebrities travel with physicians."

She ceased the wipe down and smiled sadly. "I've been explaining myself for so long…it's just habit." She shrugged. She waved the dish towel in his direction. "You can't deny that you wouldn't have been curious."

"So what if I was?" He straightened and pressed a hand to his olive-green polo. "That wouldn't have given me any right to know."

"Hmph." She leaned to pull plates from one of the bead board cabinets. "I wish more people were as respectful of privacy."

"Would you have told me if I hadn't asked about Parker?"

Kianti nodded. "I actually decided to tell you this morning. After breakfast, of course."

He frowned. "Why after breakfast?"

She laughed. "Well, I wanted you to eat before you ran out. I *did* pretty much slave over our food here, you know?"

Therin wasn't amused and let her see the agitation tighten his gorgeous features. "You figured I wouldn't stick around once you told me about your condition?"

"Men rarely do." She turned to take utensils from a drawer. "And *if* they do, it's not for long."

"I don't appreciate being put in that group, Kianti."

"Oh, don't take it seriously." Her laughter bubbled up again. "It's understandable that a man would think twice about hooking up with a woman who could die in the midst of making love."

"Jesus." Therin grimaced. "Do you ever stop to think that it's not your condition that sends a guy scramblin' but your *expectation* that he'll be an ass about it that does the trick?"

Kianti didn't have a comeback. "Would you like to eat in the kitchen or the dining room?" she asked instead.

Therin massaged the silky hair covering his head and cursed his loss of temper. Raising his head then, he watched Kianti and smiled over how smoothly it'd happened and how alive it'd made him feel when it did.

"Kitchen's fine," he said and moved to help her.

"I'm not an invalid, Therin," she snapped when he took the dishes and silverware. "I can damn well set a table—you're my guest."

In response, he took her wrist and planted her on one of the stools. "I was only offering to help, but since you *expect* me to treat you like an invalid, I'll just go on and give you what you're looking for."

Kianti's mouth parted but again she found that she had no comeback. She watched Therin set out the breakfast, giving him instruction on where to find mugs, glasses and serving utensils. While he was engaged, she indulged in observing him—looks, clothing, manner— and discovered battling with her four *over*protectors hadn't prepared her for going a round with this man. It hadn't prepared her at all.

Chapter 6

Kianti mostly picked at her food. It wasn't difficult for Therin to notice.

"I think I've been doing a pretty good job of treating you like an invalid, but I draw the line at feeding you."

Her laughter was soft, but it was there. "I rarely eat breakfast."

"Ah…bet that doesn't sit too well with your doctor." Therin spoke around a mouthful of perfectly seasoned eggs. "Could you help me out, anyway? Eating alone is almost as bad as drinking alone."

Without argument, Kianti reached for her fork and stabbed a medallion of beef sausage.

"You're a damn good cook for someone who hates eating," he complimented.

"Thanks." She ate a bit more of the sausage and gave a saucy toss of her head. "And I don't *hate* eating. It's just that my mornings start so early with practice and all…it's usually time for lunch by the time I take a break."

"Dedication indeed. Playing is certainly your passion. So does this condition run in your family?"

"My father has high blood pressure—it runs on his side of the family. But he's the only one who has the overexertion problem. Then I came along.…" She ate a bit more eggs. "In spite of my not drinking or smoking and eating right—"

"Ha! When you eat."

She raised her mug in a mock toast. "In spite of all that, *his* condition became *my* condition. What?" she asked, noticing the secretive smile he gave.

"Just that it's hard to believe that you could play so hard, that it affects your heart rate like that." The smile returned. "I wouldn't compare piano playing to running a marathon."

"Marathon? I'd never make it past the first turn." She poked fun at herself then and nodded. "But in defense of what I do, it is a very exhilarating craft and I put my all into it."

"The pills must help." He noticed her frown as if there were a bad taste in her mouth. "Kianti? The pills?" He probed. "They help, don't they?"

She pushed away her plate. "Remember what you said about not having the right to know everything?"

"I'd say you've opened the door here," he challenged and set aside his plate as well. "You've already told me so much, why stop now?"

"I stopped taking them," she blurted when it became obvious that he wasn't going to let up on the questioning.

Therin stroked a sideburn and seemed to consider

what she'd just said. "Didn't you tell me they're your only treatment?"

She scooted off the stool. "Are you done?" She took his plate without waiting for an answer.

"Did Brody take you off of them?"

"No. I took myself off them."

"What?"

She scraped any leftover food down the disposal and rinsed out the sink. "I took myself off them." She kept her back toward Therin.

"Why the hell would you do a stupid thing like that?"

In reply, Kianti began rinsing the dishes and putting them in the washer.

"Does Brody know?"

She grabbed the utensils from the kitchen island. "He does and he's fine with it."

Therin stood. "Now why don't I believe that?"

Kianti loaded the utensils. "Can we stop talking about it? I don't expect you to get it."

He blocked her way when she moved to collect more items for the dishwasher. "So help me to get it, then."

"Why do you care?" she snapped and then pressed her fingers to her temples. "I'm sorry." She went to rinse out the food warmers.

"Stop." Easily, he trapped her against the island, one hand on either side of her. "Listen, I don't know you well, but I'd like to change that."

"Why?" She kept her eyes trained on the floor. "You can't possibly be interested in pursuing a sickly woman like me."

"Maybe I am." His voice was deep and tight with emotion he realized only she had the power to rouse.

"Maybe deep down I've got some Florence Nightingale tendencies lurking." He tilted his head to study her face and saw her produce the smile he'd been seeking. He moved back to lean on the corner opposite her. "Will you at least help me understand why you'd take such a dangerous chance with your life?"

"This is almost impossible to explain to someone who's never had a chronic illness that keeps them chained to treatments." She smoothed hands across her bare arms and began to walk around the kitchen. "I want to live," she said simply. "I don't feel that I can do that with medication as a constant reminder that I'm...different."

Therin's brows drew close over his bright eyes and his heart went out to her. He caught her before she could walk past, cupping her face when he turned her to him.

"It's only one pill, sweet. Seems like a small price to pay."

Her dark gaze appeared haunted. "It's not the pills—not exactly the pills—but what they represent. Weakness. 'Kianti can't do this because she's too frail...'" she mimicked. "Do you know how many times I heard that as a child—as an adult?" She studied his face, her fingertips aching to graze the glossy sideburns framing his very handsome face. She shook off the need. "You couldn't understand," she muttered.

"You're probably right." His thumbs smoothed the flawless cinnamon of her skin before he reluctantly pulled his hands from her face. "That's probably due to selfishness, though."

Kianti brought a hand to her hip. "Selfishness?"

"I just met you and since then you've consumed the

majority of my thoughts." He invaded her space until he had her trapped against the island once more. "I don't know what the hell I'll do when I go back to Vancouver. I'm sort of getting used to seeing you every day."

"Well…" She uttered a nervous laugh, fighting to make the moment light. "It's the technology age, you know? I'm as close as your computer."

"Right." His eyes narrowed as they roamed every inch of her face. "Sadly, my laptop won't allow me to do this."

Kianti would have melted to the floor when he kissed her, had he not gathered her close before he took her mouth with his. The kiss went directly to sultry, scooping up flecks of sweetness along the way.

To accommodate for the difference in their heights, he perched her on the edge of the island and stepped between her thighs. Never once did he break the kiss. Kianti gave into the delicious tingling that began at the part of her that most ached for him and radiated outward to the rest of her. Boldly, she flexed her thighs about him and drew him closer.

Therin allowed his hands free rein, massaging her back through the cottony material of her halter. He moved around to fondle her breasts, groaning into her mouth as he squeezed.

"Mmm…" Her voice wavered when he broke the kiss to trail his mouth down her neck and across her collarbone. In moments, she felt his face at the valley between her breasts. She arched insistently, silently begging him to tend to them properly.

Therin trailed his nose down the cleft, breathing in the scent of her skin and proving to himself that her breasts were as full and supple as he'd suspected. His hands continued to fondle her, thumbs working the nipples into solid gems eager to be sucked.

"Therin…" She arched more determinedly.

The cinnamon-brown mounds nudged his mouth each time she took a breath. "Kianti…" He pressed his forehead to her chest and sighed.

"Please don't go," she easily read his mind.

Going was just what he intended on doing. Whatever was happening between them only had the chance of being a fling at best. There was, after all, a vast amount of distance between them and two very hectic lifestyles. He didn't want to accept any of it.

God, he was in trouble.

"You're afraid of me, aren't you?" Kianti asked, feeling his touch cool.

"Damn right," he admitted, and then cupped his hand about her neck when she would have looked away. "Not for the reasons you think," he said. "I've got to head back tomorrow afternoon. If I sleep with you now, I'd tell my responsibilities to go to hell."

"Would that be such a bad thing?" She kept her eyes on the massage she applied to the bend of his elbow where his sleeve ended.

"It wouldn't be bad at all." He grinned, yet rolled his eyes. "Still more of a headache than I'd need if I put it off for too long."

Kianti's mouth turned down, but she wouldn't beg. Well…no more than she already had.

"Look at me." He flexed his hand lightly about her neck and waited. "Have dinner with me tonight."

"What shall I cook?" Her dark eyes were brilliant with expectancy then.

Therin chuckled. "As much as I love your cooking, it'd be safer if we go out. Since this is your town, you pick the place."

Kianti accepted the invitation with a nod and curved her fingers into his collar. "Dress casual," she said.

"Be ready by seven." He didn't trust himself to kiss her again and simply brushed his thumb to her cheek before he left.

San Diego, California~

Former military liaison and decorated marine Shepard Yale had an unfailing reputation for being a no-nonsense, hard-as-nails leader. When Therin arrived at the corner café where he'd agreed to meet the retired general, he saw none of that spit-and-polish demeanor, but one that was more approachable. Therin assumed that becoming a grandparent definitely changed a person.

The general nodded, a smile coming to his face when he noticed Therin. He stood with a fluid grace but his posture was straight as a rod. Retired or not, the man still held on to a bit of that spit and polish.

"Hope this isn't too far out of the way, General," Therin said as they shook hands. "I got the feeling you'd want to take this meeting privately."

"I thank you for your consideration, son." Shepard Yale's mouth turned into a smile that hinted at how impressed he was. "I've heard of your diplomacy and discretion. Happy to find those attributes to be true of you."

Therin nodded. "Thank you, sir."

"Location's not a problem," the general said while reclaiming his seat at the table. "I live out in Marin now. My daughter and her family are visiting—they made a trip in to visit the Star Wars place." He shrugged. "I came along for the ride so we've got a while to chat before I have to go back to meet them."

"Well, you must know how curious I was to hear that you'd called." Therin tapped the shellacked surface of the table. "When I was an ambassador, we never had the chance to collaborate on any issues."

A waitress arrived for orders then. Once she left, General Yale studied the sunny view of the bay beyond the café's windows. "A man's issues can change with the onset of age," he said.

"Are you all right, sir?"

The general chuckled. "I'm in good health, son. Sorry for getting too prophetic on you there. I was thinking about my being a grandfather now. Perhaps the most rewarding charge I've ever had in my life. I place it above all the pomp surrounding being a liaison and decorated general, above raising my own kids, even." Something shadowed his vivid blue gaze. "I was so busy working to build my life. I devoted my time and talents to strengthening the country's infrastructure, but ignored the most basic necessities—the education of our children."

The confusion, which had lightly shadowed Therin's face for the better part of the visit, gradually cleared.

"Watching my grandkids grow, I realize I want them

to have it all or as close to getting it as they can come. Education is the foundation for making that happen."

"Agreed," Therin said just as the waitress returned with their iced teas.

"I've heard many impressive things about your work for education," the general said when they were alone again. "Your work with EYES captured my interest especially."

"Sir." Therin nodded briefly.

The general's posture softened when he leaned closer to the table. "We had our *eye* on EYES at one time. No one believed an organization raking in that kind of cash could be about as noble a cause as they claimed."

Therin grinned. "And what do you think now?"

"I think it's an organization I'd greatly like to be part of, but I'd like an insider's view before I make my intentions public."

Therin trailed his fingers along the tea glass, which had begun to sweat. "I could tell you what you already know and talk your head off about the organization's missions and successes or you could see for yourself. I'm working to put an event in place—be happy to put you on the guest list."

"Ha!" The general smacked his hand to the table. "Direct and no bullshit. Findin' more and more to like about you every minute, son."

"Sir? Offering your support this way…do you have any idea about the aggravation you're letting yourself in for?" Therin asked once their sandwiches had arrived.

General Yale laughed aloud. His weather-beaten face had taken on almost the same magenta tint as the short-sleeved dress shirt he wore. "Son, I've been in aggravations my entire career. No reason why retiring should change that."

"It's just that throwing your support toward education will set a lot of folks on edge. You're known as a hard-nosed military man whose allegiance has always been to the strengthening of our military first and foremost—everything else has appeared to have taken a backseat to that. Education, most of all." Therin shrugged while removing the pickle from his turkey club. "The ones not set on edge by you suddenly changing your stance could send a lot of their financial support toward *other* causes and away from their usual interests."

"And I'm hoping for that very thing." The general took a swallow of his tea. "I recognize the danger our kids' futures are in. In many ways I helped contribute to it. My timing's piss-poor, but I'd like to try somehow to make amends for that before I leave this place."

"General." Therin leaned across to shake the man's hand, commending his new ideals. "The event will be held in Vancouver—date is still to be determined. Should you prefer to keep your interest more discreet, I'd understand should you choose not to attend."

"Hmph. I couldn't keep it discreet if I tried. My staff works harder for me now than they did before I retired."

"I thought they'd be back in D.C. or elsewhere?" Therin took a bite of the sandwich.

"You thought right. Their superiors may have changed, but their jobs are still the same. Many of my connections, the knowledge I hold about them and how to deal with them are still of interest." He cut his roast beef on rye into quarters. "We meet from time to time to discuss such matters."

"And one thing leads to another and soon you're discussing your own…future plans?" Therin guessed, joining in when the general grinned.

"I had my staff do some checking." Shepard Yale cleared his throat as his laughter quieted. "They all told me you were the man to see for the honest scoop."

"Mmm." Therin cringed. "Having a reputation for honesty can be a negative in the political game."

"This is true." The general regarded Therin thoughtfully. "I suppose I should ask if you've thought about what sort of *aggravations* you're in store for. Bringing a hard-nosed general in on the noble bandwagon? If you didn't have enemies before, you're sure to have 'em now."

"Well, sir, it's like you said, I've been dealing with aggravations my entire career. No reason why my heading the noble bandwagon should change that."

Laughter rumbled between the two men as they raised their glasses in toast.

"I shouldn't have told you."

"Baby, please, I'm very happy, only…"

"Only you're concerned about me overdoing it."

"Well…that and…well, baby, we've sort of gotten used to being kept in the dark about the young men in your life."

Kianti smiled when her mother's words came through the phone line. The spontaneous call to her mother down in San Francisco had surprised her as well.

"Honey?" Francina Lawrence's usually robust voice held a whiff of unease.

"You're right, I…I don't know what made me call."

"He sounds special from the little you've told me."

Again, Kianti smiled, not surprised her mother caught on to her vague details regarding Therin. She felt both giddy and stupid. She was so affected by what was happening. She had to tell someone. She wouldn't acknowledge the small voice someplace deep that said she was trying to impress her mother—show her she not only had the strength to attract a good man but the will to make it last.

"So what do Brody and the guys have to say about this?"

Shadow dimmed Kianti's gaze then. "They're concerned, as usual, but I think they approve."

"And everything is still all right with Brody taking those quick pulse checks while you're on the road?"

Kianti smiled, predicting the turn a conversation with her mother usually took. "Everything's still all right, Mama."

"Your father and I would feel so much better if you'd make more time for appropriate physicals during your tour dates."

"Ma…don't, okay? I'm sorry." She winced having heard Francina's sigh over the line. "It's just that I'm feeling really good right now…please let me?"

Francina's sigh was more resigned that time. "All right, baby. All right. Can I at least tell your dad about this new young man of yours when he gets home?"

Kianti smiled, her mood brightening at thoughts of her father, Donald Lawrence. "Yes, I can't wait for you to tell him. Thanks, Mama."

"I love you, honey."

Chapter 7

Vancouver, BC, Canada~

Rick Dubose knew he had no reason to be pissed about having to head back into the office for the file he needed to finish that weekend. Still, he was pissed just the same. It wasn't every Saturday night that a man had a date with an angel.

It probably wasn't until that night, though, that his habit for being forgetful really got to him for the first time in his life.

At least he was organized. He cheered when the file was lying right where he left it on the cabinet in his cubicle.

"Jocelyn, here I come," Rick sang while stuffing the file into his satchel. He sprinted from the office, set the alarm and locked the front door. When he turned, a figure in shadow stood behind him.

"The boss is gonna get you all killed," the figure growled seconds before it eased a knife into Rick Dubose's abdomen.

Pacifica, California~

Therin was finally able to put off criticizing himself for indulging in play while there was so much work to be done. The lunch meeting with General Yale had changed all that. Productive indeed. The man's presence in EYES would reap benefits no one could imagine.

The easy expression he wore faded for a moment as all the sacrifices he'd made over the years hit home. No, his life hadn't been easy since he'd jumped on the "noble bandwagon" as the general had called it.

Such frustration, such sorrow—*loss.* He'd never admit it aloud, but it had all been due to the choices he'd made. It all combined to make him determined to see that there was something phenomenal to show for it in the end.

He shook off those heavy thoughts when Kianti's house came into view over the bend in the road. He'd grown accustomed to the nagging voice and its standard inquiry. *What the hell are you doing, Therin?*

The hell if he knew. The hell if he cared. And what about her *condition?* Did he care about that? She'd warned him that overexerting herself could prove fatal. The warning alone should have made him back off in a hurry. Instead, it only had him thinking whether he could rein in his need for her when they made love. For they certainly would make love. That much, he'd settled in his mind.

Casey O'Dell waved while pressing the button to engage the gate leading to Kianti's place. Therin parked the gleaming silver Chrysler 300 and headed toward Casey for handshakes. Now used to Therin's visits, Casey didn't bother to ring for his mistress and let her familiar guest up on the elevator.

Casa Marvelo was a romantic Mexican restaurant not far from Kianti's place in Pacifica. The food was to die for, but it was the ambience Kianti was going for that evening. Therin would be leaving on Sunday and... what? She was going to pull out all the stops to get him into her bed.

She set the lotion on the dresser with more force than necessary while wishing herself luck with that. *Tons of luck,* especially since she'd already told him about her illness. While he played the role of a man who didn't scare easily, she knew it was only a matter of time. God, how she wanted him....

Throwing up her hands and forgetting about her *wants,* she inspected herself in the dresser mirror and the floor-length one next to her bed. A frown rumbled her brow when she stepped closer to the mirror. She angled herself to and fro as if somehow the movements would make the run in her stockings disappear.

Cursing, she took a seat on the bed and tugged up the hem of the cranberry wrap dress to see how high the snag went.

"Damn." She glimpsed her watch and then speed-walked to the dresser to select a fresh, and hopefully run-free pair of hose. She unfastened the spike-heeled pumps and removed the damaged garments, tossing them to the nightstand.

She bit her lip and hesitated before slipping on the new pair. Debating then, she trailed her nails across her bare thighs. The night may've been warm enough to go without. Biting her lip, she went to the windows and unhinged the lock to push open one side and take in the fragrant sea air kissed with a hint of warmth.

Might be all right, she told herself. Besides, if seduction was the order of the evening, hose would only be an obstacle. Satisfied by that train of thought, a saucy smirk curved her mouth and she turned from the window and right into Therin.

"Guess Casey didn't ring up." The smile he wore radiated no humor.

Kianti felt her lashes flutter and bowed her head to order them to stop. She cast a quick glance and wave toward the open window. "I was just about to put on my hose."

Therin eliminated any personal space existing between them. "What for?"

Her effort to find a response was unnecessary. He was kissing her then and the only things leaving her mouth were moans. She went to her toes, seeking as much height as she could gain in order to enjoy his kiss more comfortably—in order to feel the unyielding length of his frame more adequately.

Therin handled that when he tugged her high against him and backed her next to the closest wall. Without shame, Kianti wrapped her legs around his back and returned his kiss with a fiery eagerness.

There was the nagging voice again at the back of Therin's mind but the whispers coming from Kianti's throat silenced them easily.

Her fingers found the buttons along his collarless wine-colored shirt and made quick work of them. She whimpered amidst the kiss while raking her nails across the steely expanse of his chest that was bared to her touch where the shirt hung open. She ended the kiss to outline the cleft in his chin with the tip of her tongue. Then she began a feast upon his earlobe. "Take me to my bed," she whispered.

Her words were like part of some hypnotic suggestion he had no choice but to obey. They were on the bed seconds later. The kiss resumed yet broke on a curse when Therin acknowledged he had no weapons against her. He had the controlling position sprawled across her small, trembling form but it was she who commanded whatever move he sought to make.

She drove her tongue erotically against his. Her lips curved into a half smile when she heard his groans and felt the tension ease from his body. She arched herself into a bow, tossing her arms above her head.

"Undress me...."

Therin closed his eyes tightly as if to ward off her instruction. It was a hopeless waste of time.

As if to prompt him to do her bidding, she drew her thumbnail across his nipple and suckled his tongue at the initiation of another kiss.

"Undress me, Therin...."

He told himself that he wouldn't hurt her. He could take it—take *her* slow. He had to because he had to have her.

Kianti tugged her lip between her teeth as she was claimed by a wave of elation. The determination on his gorgeous face told her that he was done denying himself. The fact that she was about to be treated to what she'd been denying *herself* was enough to make her scream with delight.

Therin had undone the ties to her dress in a matter of seconds. His nose blazed a trail across her collarbone, the swells of her breasts and the fragrant valley between. When he spotted the front clasp of her bra, his shaft nudged the button fly of his dark trousers. One easy flick of his thumb and it came apart releasing the full, pert mounds to his gaze…to his mouth.

Again, his nose blazed the trail, outlining the shape of her cleavage. He paid special attention to the nipple steadily firming beneath his manipulations.

"Put me in your mouth," she ordered seconds before he did it.

Therin couldn't help but liken himself to some inexperienced kid taking direction with an eager mind and body. He should have felt offended, instead he'd never felt more alive.

Kianti lost the ability to offer any further direction when he took the nipple and suckled with a deft finesse. She continued to writhe beneath him, arching shamelessly and on fire to feel every bit of him.

Expert fingers manipulated one nipple while perfect teeth bit down softly on its twin. Moments later, Therin switched to the other nipple and molested it in much the same fashion. He tugged the open front of her dress farther apart, and eased a hand beneath her back. He lifted her slightly to pull away every scrap of clothing clinging to her body.

Kianti moaned her disappointment when his mouth traveled away from the wet nipple. His nose dipped into her belly button just briefly before moving down to explore the baby-hair-smattered triangle above her sex. Her legs quivered noticeably as she arched more uncontrollably.

Therin was of a mind then to torture and in the most sensual manner. His nose outlined her clit and labia. His smile was arrogance personified when she hiccupped on the gasp she uttered. He held her still, strong hands curved about her thighs before his tongue replaced his nose. That time, she hiccupped his name and twined her fingers in her hair loose and flowing around her oval face.

Her scent enticed him like a drug. It clung to every part of her—most of all, the part of her he was especially infatuated with just then. His tongue plunged deep. He had to know if she tasted as incredible as she smelled.

Better, he thought when his tongue sank into an abundance of heat and moisture. He applied a warning squeeze to her toned thighs when her hips lifted from the tangled bed. Slowly, she thrust against his mouth and cursed the orgasmic waves that sliced through her. She wanted to savor and savor…what he was doing felt far too incredible to be hurried.

Therin pleasured her tirelessly, jerking out of his shirt and dark jacket as he did so. Kianti watched him, her ebony eyes half open and glistening with desire. The flex of the muscles in his back and shoulders was as powerful an aphrodisiac as his tongue rotating inside her. She smoothed her palms across his head, luxuriating in the close-cut waves that rivaled his skin for silken appeal.

He could feel her inner walls tense and knew she'd be coming in moments. It was then that he focused on her reaction—searching for any signs of discomfort. The bliss on her exquisite face served to stoke his ego as opposed to his concern. He worked kisses upward again ignoring her hypnotic voice when she told him she wanted more. Instead, he took hold of her bare bottom and drew her into him.

"I want this," she groaned, circling her sex against the thick bulge still confined within his trousers. "Mmm...I want this." The words silenced and they nuzzled into another kiss. "Mmm..." She took great pleasure and time in drawing her moisture from his tongue. The kiss lasted but a few heated seconds before Therin pulled back suddenly.

Kianti blinked. "I'm fine," she promised.

He smiled yet shook his head while frowning. "I didn't come prepared...no condoms." He grimaced over the admission.

Kianti tilted her head and looked up and over at the nightstand. "Check the drawer."

The regret in his crystalline stare shimmered into what Kianti would have sworn was anger. "I was hoping we'd come back after dinner and...I hadn't planned on taking no for an answer." She bit her lip and awaited his reaction.

He looked down at her chest heaving and fondled a nipple until she moaned. "Would you have taken me against my will, Ms. Lawrence?"

"Mmm...are you trying to...entrap me, Mr. Ambassador?" She winced on the pleasure of his touch.

"In a manner of speaking," he answered. Taking her

wrists, he held them above her head and plied her with another languid kiss.

"Therin, please…give me this." She ground herself desperately against him.

He rose up then, leaving the bed to unfasten his belt and trousers. They joined the shoes and socks on the carpet along with his boxers.

Kianti had pushed herself up toward the head of the bed. She braced on her elbows and watched the garments fall. No desire was masked in her tilting onyx stare until her lashes settled and she moaned in expectation of the ecstasy she was sure to find with his flawlessly sculpted frame.

Therin kissed his way back up her body. Once more, he stopped to pay homage to her breasts. Kianti shuddered at the graze of his arousal, stiff and lengthy against her thigh. Again, she begged him. He kissed her to silence further pleas while wrenching open the nightstand drawer and rooting around inside for what he needed.

Kianti linked her arms about his neck, brushing her nipples across the taut, muscled breadth of his chest. Her nails grazed the carved pecs and abs on a journey downward until she closed her hand just barely around the width of him.

It was Therin who begged that time when she began stroking him into another level of hardness. Falling victim to sensation, his head fell to her shoulder and he moved helplessly against her hand.

The nagging voice warned Therin that he was dangerously close to coming. He took heed and moved away reluctantly to set the condom in place.

"Shh…" Kianti placed two fingers across his mouth before he could take time to reassure her.

Once more, she felt the potent grip of his hands on her thighs. Soon after, she felt the wide head of his sex probing her entrance. He eased in slow, going deeper until she gloved him to the hilt.

Therin closed his eyes on the sinful tightness sheathing him in a haven of creamy warmth. He called on every ounce of restraint he possessed. The promises he'd made to go slow with her seemed hollow then. All he could think of was taking her any way he could and having the curvaceous cinnamon beauty at his beck and call.

Kianti had no thoughts on exercising restraint. She moved on him with a recklessness that held her oblivious to anything else. Therin couldn't help but match her passion. Their groans and hushed words of seduction filled the room.

She curved her hands about the posts lining her headboard and added renewed vigor to her movements. Therin muttered something incomprehensible before cupping a bouncing breast.

He manipulated, suckled and grazed it with his teeth. A measure of arrogance fueled him, driven by the feel of her tightness giving way as he carved his own unique place inside her.

Kianti was greedy for all he had to give, but the approaching climax commanded her surrender. Therin shuddered above her as he came seconds later. For an eternity, it seemed, they lay in a tangle of covers, arms and legs. Therin was first to move, roused by the thundering of Kianti's heart.

Chapter 8

"Are you all right?"

She nodded. "Yes, very." She smiled. "Therin, I've never felt better."

Still, he searched her face for a full five seconds.

Kianti's dark eyes sparked as she followed the path of her hand across his cheek. "I'll be even better when you give me more."

"Forget it." He had the audacity to smirk.

Her mood soured instantly. The sparkling of her eyes became a glitter of rising anger.

"I have a feeling that was way more exertion than you needed."

Kianti rolled her eyes. "I assure you it wasn't." She wouldn't allow herself to harp on any possibility that she'd overexerted herself.

"Well," he groaned while turning onto his back, "I'm pooped."

Again, Kianti rolled her eyes away from the arousing image of him lying there stroking his chiseled abs. "I knew you'd do this," she hissed, turning over and propping her fist upon a pillow. "Have a taste, and then run like a scared little boy afterward," she clarified when he looked over at her. She would have left the bed, but he grabbed her wrist so suddenly, she'd scarcely seen him move.

"Do you think that's all I intend to have of you?" His expression was hard.

Kianti didn't know how to respond and only lowered her gaze.

"Stopping just now was as much for your benefit as it was for mine."

She stiffened. "Were you holding back?"

Again, he smiled. "At the risk of making you mad, yes."

Her laughter was brief and humorless after she uttered a curse.

"Do you want me to go?"

"No, dammit, I want you to stay here and make love with me again." Her reply came without a moment's hesitation.

Therin's chuckle filled the bedroom. "You're killing me…"

"I think you're confusing yourself with me," she snapped.

"Maybe." He braced his weight to an elbow. "But as you've been dishing out 'requests' all night, I guess that entitles me to one of my own."

Her ebony gaze narrowed.

"Sleep with me."

She melted, wanting to hold on to her frustration but finding that she couldn't. "Are you sure about sleeping over? You might wake up to find me taking what I want from you."

Therin nodded, gazing in wonder at the coarse dark locks that tumbled across her back. "I'll keep that in mind."

She nodded. "So long as I'm understood. I'm not a woman who beats around the bush waiting to be offered what I want." Something haunting crept into her eyes then. "I know how fragile life is and I don't intend on wasting any of it *waiting.*"

He toyed with a tendril of her hair, twisting it about his index finger before he met her stare. "I get it, Kia. Now will you sleep with me?"

The rich tone of his voice, mingled with the sweetness of his words and the shortening of her name, were Kianti's undoing. She snuggled down next to him. Both were asleep in seconds—neither stirred for the rest of the night.

Therin was first to wake the next morning. He dressed and started coffee before returning to the bedroom. From his position against the doorjamb, he studied Kianti for a long while.

At first, he was simply taken in by the sight of her tousled and naked but for the sheet twisted around her lovely brown body. He finally had an answer for the nagging voice consistently asking what he thought he was doing. He was falling in love with the tiny, talented beauty he'd enjoyed the pleasures of the night before.

The words gave him pause. Had last night evoked the

sudden feelings of love? He'd bet everything he owned that it hadn't. He'd been falling, cautiously but surely, perhaps from the moment he'd met her.

She began to stir beneath the gray woven coverings and Therin braced off the jamb. He took a seat on the edge of the bed and leaned near, draping an arm across her prone form. Gently, he reached out to smooth a few locks of hair from her thoroughly kissed mouth. The top sheet was bunched loosely at her breasts, beckoning him to indulge. He let his fingers be nudged by the gradual heaving of her bosom as she breathed.

He'd done his best to mask the fear in his voice and expression over the frantic sound of her heartbeat. He thought back to what she'd said about taking herself off the pills and the anger he'd felt then returned in a sudden wave. What the hell was that doctor of hers thinking?

Kianti woke as if on cue and Therin forgot everything else while drowning in the sleepy dark pools of her gaze. A disturbed current eased into her stare as she took note of the clothes he wore.

"You're going?"

"Only for a few hours." His deep voice was soft while he stroked her temple. "There's a meeting I need to go to."

Kianti propped herself on an elbow. She took in the sudden agitation which flashed on his handsome face.

"Can I at least make you breakfast?" she asked instead of questioning the look.

"I'll grab something while I'm out." He dropped a quick kiss to her mouth and stood. "This is my cell number." He waved a card between his index and middle finger before pressing it to the nightstand. "Call if you need anything before I get back."

Realizing it was pointless to argue, she snuggled her head into the pillow. "'Kay."

He graced her with a wink and a smile before leaving the room.

Therin didn't bother to put a smile in place when he spotted the four men across the café dining room. He greeted them with nods and handshakes and they all placed breakfast orders before getting to the point of the meeting.

"This is about Kianti," Cube David guessed from his position at the opposite end of the rectangular table.

"That's right." Therin nodded.

"And if you're here, that means she's told you who *he* really is," Winton Terry noted, glancing toward the man who sat next to him.

Again, Therin nodded while looking toward Brody. "In light of that, I don't see how any doctor worth a damn could allow his patient to self-medicate or in this case, *not* medicate."

Brody smiled, but waited until the server had set out milk for Cube and coffees for the rest, to the table. "If you know that, then you already know at least two other things about our lovely Kianti." He dropped his elbows to the faux-wood-grained table. "She hates those pills with a passion and she's not a woman who appreciates being told what she can't do."

"To hell with that," Therin growled, though he fully understood Brody's words. "You're her doctor. One she trusts enough to have travel with her." He waved a hand across the table before laying it down. "You tell her there's no wiggle room on that—take it or leave it."

The rest of the guys exchanged glances before joining in on a round of soft laughter.

Khan tugged up the sleeves of his sweatshirt and cleared his throat over the remnants of his laughter. "You've obviously never tried to tell her what she *can't* do."

Therin wasn't amused. "This is her life we're talkin' about."

"Now hold on, man." Cube pointed a finger in Therin's direction. "Don't mistake us. We care about Key's welfare more than we do our own, but when it comes to this medical stuff…" He shrugged. "We take our cues from Bro. If he's cool with lettin' her do this, we've got to believe he knows she'll come through it okay."

"Forgive me if I don't share your certainty." Therin massaged the bridge of his nose.

"By my calculation you've only known her a little over a week." Winton toyed with the rolled cuff of his sleeve. "Already such concern…"

Therin's smile emerged slowly. His light stare was dangerously probing as he regarded Winton. "What does that tell you?"

Winton waited as their breakfast orders arrived. He glanced toward his colleagues then. "That tells me you've been charmed as totally and as easily as every other man who meets her."

Therin smiled, looking down at his platter, but didn't dig in. "You're chalking my concern up to momentary fascination," he told Winton.

"No man is *momentarily* fascinated with Key," Khan said after washing down his food with a mouthful of juice.

"She hasn't had a serious relationship in a few years…that's why," Winton said. "Every man who meets her realizes she's no momentary fascination. Unfortunately, that condition of hers rears its ugly head sooner or later and she has to choose between being happy and being alive."

"But dammit, that's not a choice she has to make," Therin snapped.

"It's not just about taking a pill," Khan said. "It's what the pills represent for her. She thinks of them as a badge of shame. She's been tied to them her entire life. She's a strong-willed person and to be…dependent on them is probably harder on her than the illness itself."

"Christ." Therin pushed away his untouched plate, nodding toward Cube when he requested permission to dive in.

For the next five minutes, Therin watched them passing salt and sharing food. He studied them each closely and eventually realization dawned.

"You're waiting her out, aren't you?"

"If it seems like a cop out, it is." Brody spoke up then. "I'm not happy about it one damn bit, but to argue with her over it would aggravate things more than they already have been." He bowed his head and massaged the area where his Afro tapered at the neck. "It terrifies me to think about her off of her medication."

The clatter of silverware and glasses slowly diminished as the rest of the guys stilled. Before now, none of them had heard Brody voice that particular concern.

"I told her we'd be watching her like a hawk…if something happened, I'd insist on her forgetting this foolishness and begin her regimen again. I'm confident she'll take them if she needs them. I have to be."

Therin cursed and buried his face in his hands as he inhaled deeply to cool his temper. The others seemed to lose their appetites as well.

Khan was first to stand. "I'll get the check. Catch you guys later. Mr. Rucker." He nodded a goodbye.

"Yeah, I'm outta here, too. Got some stuff to do." Cube followed next. "Rucker," he bid.

"Good seeing you again, Rucker." Winton extended a hand to shake.

"Give us a minute, man," Brody said when the waiter came to collect dishes. "Have you two slept together?" he asked once the young waiter had walked on.

Therin propped a sneaker-shod foot to the chair Winton had vacated. Bracing a fist to his forehead, the resigned smile he gave was confirmation enough.

"How was she when you left her?" Brody asked.

A muscle danced along Therin's jaw as it tightened. "She was sleeping, woke up before I left. Said she wanted to make me breakfast." He smiled briefly on the memory.

Brody picked at his bacon. "Did she tell you about her condition before or after you…?"

"Before."

"And I suppose you figured you could…keep yourself in check around her?"

"The hell with you, doc." Therin's fist landed on the table. "I didn't jump on her the second I met her. Hell, I didn't even want to risk it—"

"Exactly." Brody straightened in his chair. "May I speak frankly?"

Therin's laughter drew a fair amount of attention. "Isn't that what we've been doing?"

Brody grinned. "Khan was right. What he said about not being able to tell her what to do. She's got a way… an almost undetectable way of working things in her favor."

"That passion of hers?" Brody waited for Therin's nod. "It's evident in all she does. *All,* Mr. Ambassador."

The muscle began its wicked dance along Therin's jaw again. "Are you speaking from experience, then?"

"No. Not mine—others." Brody ran his hand across the low afro. "Key's last relationship was over three years ago. Things didn't move nearly as fast there as they have with the two of you but they made progress. The first night they slept together, she wound up in the ER."

Therin went cold beneath his tan hoody.

"Hmph. The guy could've used time in the ER himself—he looked ready to pass out." Brody smiled. "I think he did when Cube got there."

"What kind of idiot do you think I am? You believe I'd intentionally overlook the risk and put her in danger?"

Brody leaned forward, clasping his hands against the top of the table. "No. I don't think that, and neither did her last two acquaintances—but it happened." His voice softened. "What I'm saying is that in spite of best intentions, I don't know a man alive who could take it slow and easy with a woman like that."

Therin's words had failed then and he offered no argument.

Brody regarded him for a moment before he stood. "I'd appreciate you not mentioning our chat with Kianti. She'd kill us slow if she knew we'd talked to you."

When silence met his request, Brody sighed and left the table.

The waiter returned to clear the dishes, noticed the harsh look Therin wore and decided to return once the table was vacant.

Therin stared unseeingly past the windows and wondered if it was too late to shut down emotion and back off from Kianti Lawrence. A host of responses filtered his brain—all of them telling him he was already hopelessly beyond the point of no return. He had never opened himself up to such a rush of emotion. In spite of the many women he'd known before, he'd never *wanted* to open himself up to such emotion. His fate was sealed, he knew it and he'd passed the point of caring.

He felt the phone vibrate in his jean pocket and quickly checked to see if it was her. The sight of Vaughn's name on the faceplate brought a frown to his face and he pushed the phone back into his pocket. He remained at the table for another half hour.

Chapter 9

The final phrase of the adagio silenced in the screened porch overlooking the sea. Kianti kept her second Baby Grand there and used that area for creating the bulk of her original pieces. After Therin's sudden departure earlier that morning, she'd showered and headed out to the porch to...test herself.

The fact that her activities with Therin Rucker hadn't kept her passed out in bed for the remainder of the day gave her hope that change might be on the horizon. She spent the next two hours working at the piano and felt stronger instead of exhausted.

When the rush of ocean waves filled the area with sound, Kianti closed her eyes and wondered if she was lying to herself. To prove or rather *dis*prove it, she set out to focus—attempting to lock in on any sign of weakness or overexertion. She felt nothing negative and prayed the lilt of excitement beneath her breast would be the first of many.

She wouldn't push it, she promised herself and scanned the row of piano keys beneath her fingertips. Hmph, she thought. It'd be damned impossible to keep that vow, especially now.

She'd never done anything so bold as to go without the medication she'd taken since childhood. The possibility of success looming near was something she wanted to eagerly embrace instead of approach with caution.

The touch of fingers between her shoulder blades, left bare by the low back of the mosaic-print lounge robe, stirred another excited lilt below her breast. The incredible cologne Therin wore drifted past her nose and set her mind on memories of their erotic evening together.

"Play something for me," he asked, settling next to her on the long gray cushioned bench.

After a moment's thought to the piece she wanted, Kianti obliged. Her performance was admirable considering her true focus rested on what his hands and mouth were doing to her. They moved slowly, but with a definite purpose as his fingers strummed their own tune along her spine. One hand circled her waist in search of a front opening to the robe.

Kianti gave herself up to the sensation of the moment. Closing her eyes, she allowed it to overwhelm her.

"Keep playing for me," he taunted when her fingers fumbled over the keys.

Mercilessly, he caressed her to distraction. Kianti's fingers faltered more as the piece neared closing. She gave in to the need swelling within her. Therin was weighing a breast while his thumb brushed the nipple with a touch so light it may have been imagined. She practically sizzled beneath it. Her head fell back against his shoulder as the notes silenced.

"Don't stop…" she urged when his touch traveled her thighs—higher until he was stroking her with a rich intensity that had her arching shamelessly against him. "Mmm…" She bit her lip on the sensation his middle finger evoked as it rotated deep inside her.

Therin nibbled her earlobe then and subjected her to a triple caress that had her turning into his arms moments later. Without effort, he scooped her petite form across his lap. He made her straddle him as he kissed her. Kianti locked her arms about his neck and drove her tongue hungrily against his. She shivered again feeling the air touch her bare skin when he tugged the robe from her shoulders.

The scene there on the sun-drenched porch lasted several seductive moments before Therin took her up with him and on to the bedroom.

"Hurry…" she moaned once he had her on the bed and was slowly peeling away the rest of the robe.

Therin ignored the order, preferring to take his time completing the task. He brushed his mouth across every part of her body he bared to his brilliant stare.

Kianti did her best to free him of his clothes. Difficult, considering every part of her was weakened by his attention. Eventually though, Therin was definitely as affected as she was. Raising above her, he practically ripped the hoody and undershirt from his back. Meanwhile, Kianti took care of his belt and jean unfastening.

"Hell…" Therin remembered and jerked open the nightstand drawer for a condom. As he searched for what he wanted, Kianti nibbled the angle of his jaw and cupped his sex.

Then it was Therin who had become weak. He groaned and settled his handsome face in the crook of her neck to savor the feel of her hand moving up and down his length. Kianti took care of slipping the condom in place, an act which aroused him even more.

Split seconds later, he was inside her and squeezing his eyes shut tightly as he mentally chanted the phrase—*slowly…* Again, he buried his face in her neck and tried to follow the order.

Kianti made another helpless sound of need and tried to push Therin to his back. He wouldn't allow it.

"I want to be on top." Weakly, she pounded her fists against his flexing pecs. "Please let me ride you."

"Please shut up," he groaned just as his tongue filled her mouth and he lost the ability to restrain himself.

He drew her leg across his shoulder. The added penetration was enough to silence Kianti as far as it related to issuing any demands.

Therin felt his concern ebb when the rapid thudding of her heart began to slow.

"What was that you played for me out there?" He kissed the top of her untidy head.

"'Stolen Moment,'" she said following a second's hesitation, and focused in on her thumbnail grazing his collarbone.

"Is it yours?"

"I actually just wrote it—since we met."

Therin heard her sigh and he frowned. He cupped her chin until she looked up at him. "What?"

"Nothing." She took advantage of the moment to straddle him.

He took her wrists and squeezed. "What?"

Lying down atop him, she snuggled close. "That's what this feels like—a stolen moment. Like we're taking something we have no right to. With all of our responsibilities, *my* health issues, which have always made me feel that love and passion weren't for me... Sometimes I feel like it could all be taken back." She forced a laugh when he kissed her head again. "I hope I haven't scared you by telling you that?"

"Not a bit." Silently, he admitted that her words mirrored his feelings to a T.

"Therin?" She hesitated and smiled when he jostled her slightly to urge her to continue. "I think this is something I'd fight like hell to keep for as long as I can." She scooted up to meet his kiss when he tugged.

Kianti shook her head while scrolling down through her PDA. "Can't believe I forgot this... A group at this club has a vocal trio out of New Jersey performing with them tonight." She turned to fix Therin with apology in her tilting gaze. "They asked me months ago to sit in on piano."

Therin was already grinning as he watched her from the armchair he occupied. "It's not a problem. I like Scottie's. You don't mind if I tag along, do you?"

Kianti let the PDA hang limp in her hand. "Scottie's?"

"Unless your drummer friend would mind if you

bring a guest along." He winked and pushed out of the chair.

Kianti leaned back on her dresser. "How did you—?"

"I didn't catch his name when I was there before."

"Why didn't you tell me?"

Therin shrugged. "Well, I had them send you a drink. What'd they give you, by the way?"

Kianti slapped his bare shoulder when he leaned next to her against then dresser. "Why didn't you come and say hello to me?"

"I was debating."

"On?"

He bowed his head. "Whether to tell you I was there, 'specially after I saw you with your friend."

"Shelton?"

Therin's sleek brows rose. "You guys seemed pretty close."

Kianti nudged his shoulder. "Are you jealous?"

"Should I be?"

"No." She laughed.

"Does your boy Shelton know that?"

It was Kianti's turn to shrug then. "I guess so." She smiled when he fingered the strap that had slid from her shoulder when she shrugged. "We've known each other a long time. Most we've ever talked about at length is our passion—music." She folded her arms across the bodice of the lilac lounge dress she wore. "He's one of the musicians I'm working with on the school I told you about."

"I remember." Therin let his eyes trail her bare skin in a blatantly lurid manner. "I'll bet he really enjoys those conversations."

Kianti threw her head back and laughed. "You're crazy! Besides, there's no chance for a love affair with my *drummer friend* anyway."

"Because he's gay?" Therin's tone was hopeful.

She smirked. "Because of *you*."

"Me?"

Her gaze faltered. "You've got a little something to do with it."

"A little something?" he challenged, bringing his mouth to her ear and beginning a soft nibble of the silky skin beneath it. Kianti tilted her head, offering his mouth more room to roam.

In one smooth, effortless move, Therin clutched her waist and pulled her from the dresser. Keeping her captive between his thighs, he cupped his hands around her neck and propped his thumbs beneath her jaw to bring her chin up for his kiss.

A shuddery moan lilted from deep in her throat when his tongue enticed hers to a wet, passionate romp. Kianti linked her arms about his neck and brushed her firming nipples against his chest.

Therin squeezed her hips, bringing her closer to the part of him that was hung low and hard for her.

Kianti felt the proof of desire below his sleep pants and knew there would be no going anywhere except to bed if she didn't resist…or at least *try* to.

"I've got to get in the shower now if I intend to get to the club at a decent time." She groaned when he ignored her and brought his hands round to cup and fondle her breasts. "You're welcome to share it with me.…"

Therin looked at her then as though she had lost

her mind. "Do you really intend to keep this date?" he asked, joining in when she laughed.

"These people can get pretty wild, but they're a great bunch," Kianti warned Therin as they made their way into Scottie's through the back entrance.

Therin grimaced playfully while holding open the door for her. "Do you think I'm some kind of stick-in-the-mud because of my profession?"

"Well, these folks aren't a group of educators," she drawled and tugged on the sleeve of the black denim jacket he wore.

"Key Law in da house!" a pencil-slim man in a chef's hat bellowed when he spotted the new arrivals in his kitchen.

"Hey, Nate." Kianti giggled when the man tugged her into a bear hug. "Nate Eastman, this is Therin Rucker. Nate is Scottie's head chef and one of the most sought after chefs in California."

"Cali!" Nate feigned offense. "Hell, the world! What's up, man?" he said, extending a hand for Therin to shake.

"Havin' your usual, Key?" Nate's second in command Anton Sewell asked from his place behind a big stove.

"Yeah, thanks Ant!" Kianti waved toward Therin who was still talking with Nate. "Would you like a salad?" she asked when he looked over. "Scottie's has the best in town."

"My kitchen connections are what convinced Cube to come on board as my security," Kianti told Therin once they were fixed up with huge chef's salads and on their way out of the kitchen. Their laughter traveled down the winding corridor they took.

The dressing room at Scottie's was a huge place only sectioned off inside by privacy screens for those who felt the need to use them.

The group was definitely a bawdy one, but they all welcomed Therin like he was one of them. The gang was even more intrigued by the newcomer once Khan announced that Therin was a former ambassador. Drinks and conversation flowed, but Therin took advantage of the time to study the dynamics of Kianti and her crew.

He watched her and Khan discuss what style she'd wear her hair that evening. Therin loved the way the heavy coarse mass cascaded behind her shoulders when Khan raked his fingers through it. He looked on while Winton spoke with her about a license agreement for one of her CDs. A data company was interested in hosting it for distribution to libraries nationwide. Cube fetched her more salad while Brody checked her pulse rate.

Therin couldn't help but wonder as he regarded the unorthodox family. With all that male presence in her life, did Kianti Lawrence have room for more?

For the next few days, Therin and Kianti set out to add memories to their stolen moments.

They enjoyed everything: morning and moonlit walks along the beach; several firelit dinners were enjoyed there as well. As the waves ebbed, they talked and learned more about one another.

Those conversations steered clear of anything that could bring shadow to their bliss. Taboo topics were of course Kianti's condition, as well as Therin's schedule. They avoided that subject especially, knowing the time was right there and bearing down on them. He had to go and it was the last thing either of them wanted.

"I said no, Kia."

Kianti bit down hard on his earlobe. "If I didn't know better I'd swear you have a thing about control." She felt his laughter vibrate against her ear.

"Don't all men?" he inquired.

"Mmm…well, thankfully, I haven't had the pleasure of dealing with many who'd turn down the chance to lie back and be pleasured."

He kept his eyes closed as a smile emerged. "Should that comfort me?"

"It should shame you into letting me…" Lying partially beneath him, she nudged herself against the provocative bulge below his sleep pants. "I'm used to having a fair amount of control in the bedroom."

Therin massaged the bridge of his nose but that did nothing to take his mind off the increasing stiffness of his shaft. They were wrapped in a cozy fleece on the living room sofa where they'd come to watch the sunrise on a chilly morning.

Not long after the sun had claimed its position in the sky, did Kianti make her play for another seductive scene starring herself in the lead role. Therin shut down her every attempt, which mattered little, as evidence of his desire was unmistakable.

She engaged him in a sultry kiss, arching erotically

against him and moaning quietly as she suckled his tongue into her mouth. "Let me on top? You'd still be in control, you know?" She kissed him hungrily before she eased back a tad. "You're so…strong and I'm just a little ol' thing. If I get too wild, you can just pull me off." She shrugged and ground her hips against him. "No effort at all."

"Will you please?" he groaned, taking charge of the kiss then because he craved it and because her taunting was driving him insane.

Therin's phone was on the coffee table. Its vibrating hum against the wood was ignored. It stopped, and then resumed again seconds later. Still…ignored. Barely a minute passed, then the phone on the end table began to ring.

The couple shot a murderous glare toward the cordless.

"It's Casey." Kianti recognized the number from the security booth when she checked the cordless faceplate.

"Are you expecting anybody?" he asked while kissing at her neck.

"No. Are you?" she asked when the cordless stopped ringing and Therin's vibrated again.

He leaned across her to grab the phone. "Damn."

"I take that as a yes?" She smiled.

"Can't be," he muttered when the cordless started ringing again.

"Let's find out." She clicked on the phone. "Hi, Casey…mmm-hmm. Yes, just a sec—" She looked to Therin. "Vaughn Burgess."

The mood was effectively ruined. Therin growled something incomprehensible and left the sofa.

"The bastards threaten me with bodily harm when I don't take time for myself, and when I do they won't let me have it," he ranted. "Where the hell are my shoes?"

Kianti wouldn't dare tell him how adorable he was to her then. "Casey? Tell Mr. Burgess that Mr. Rucker will be right down." She set the phone aside and wrapped herself tighter in the blanket. "Maybe it's not that big of a deal."

"It is," he grumbled, tugging on the sneakers he'd left beneath the coffee table the night before. "I've been ignoring his calls all week."

She pulled him down for a kiss before he could walk past. "The sooner you see to it, the sooner you can get back."

Therin lingered near, savoring the momentary closeness. He didn't tell her how much he doubted her words.

Vaughn met Therin with his hands raised in a defensive hold. He apologized once the distance closed between them in the wide drive outside the house.

"I can't think of one reason good enough for you to bother me here." Therin's eyes sparked with a hazel fire.

Vaughn got right to the point. "Rick was stabbed last Saturday night."

Therin stilled, and then he gave a quick shake of his head and a smile which noted that it must have been *him* who was hearing weird things. "Did you just—?"

"Rick Dubose was stabbed last Saturday night," Vaughn repeated.

Therin watched his friend for another long minute, then he went to lean against the Jeep Vaughn had driven out to Kianti's.

"I'm guessing this wasn't a mugging?" He stroked his jaw.

Vaughn shook his head. "It was intentional."

"How is he?"

"Stable. Nothing vital was hit. But they aren't letting anyone other than family in for visits just now."

"And we know this was intentional because?"

"Rick heard the guy say his boss was gonna get him killed."

"Call Morgan. Tell him to release the staff until further notice."

"Therin, I don't—"

"Vaughn? I don't want to hear anything but 'okay.'"

"Okay. *But.*" He raised his hands. "That's not going to make this go away."

"Course it isn't." Therin left the Jeep and turned toward the ocean view. "I'm just making it easier for the sons of bitches. They seem content takin' the coward's route—going after my staff." He shrugged. "Once they're out of the way, the jackasses can come after me. Stop all this pissin' around. They want me to share the wealth, encourage our members to not be so generous with their donations, send them on to other worthwhile causes such as their own? I say no."

"Dammit, T, do you hear what you're sayin'?" Vaughn walked around to look Therin in the face. "Rick was stabbed. This has gotten physical. I think it's fair to say your enemies might be so set on tamping down your philanthropic efforts, that they'd be willing to kill you to do it."

"So be it." Therin's jaw clenched as he spoke the words.

"T—"

"I don't wanna hear it."

Vaughn bowed his head, and then nodded toward the house towering in the distance. "And what about her?"

"What about her?" Therin's glare turned deadly.

Vaughn didn't lose his nerve. "This crusade of yours could get you killed. I'd say that'd be an effective relationship ender."

Therin wouldn't comment on that. "I spoke to the general since I've been here," he shared instead.

"Details," Vaughn asked, his eyes narrowing.

Therin quickly recapped the highlights from his talk with Shepard Yale. He shrugged. "There's no turning back, V. The general becoming the newest member of EYES is going to rock some pretty solid foundations. I'm guessing that the same folks behind my present difficulties are the same ones who won't look too kindly on the general supporting my…crusade."

Vaughn's confusion cleared. "You're trying to get them to reveal themselves?" He shoved his hands into the pockets of his sweatpants and glared. "You're insane. People like this don't come out from behind the curtain, Ther. They send others to do their bidding. Even if you *did* find out who they are, do you really think they're the *only* ones who oppose you?"

"Guess we're about to find out how asinine my plan is, then." Therin walked over to clap Vaughn's shoulder. "The general wants to use the Vancouver event to announce his support for the organization, which is big considering his reputation. He's spent his life focused on building a powerful military. To now say education is more important…do you know how many others that could influence?"

"Jesus." Vaughn massaged a sudden ache at the base of his neck. "So what are you gonna do?" he asked when he saw Therin looking toward Kianti's house.

Therin's fist clenched. "The last thing I want to."

Chapter 10

Though the majority of the plans for the EYES fund-raiser had been handled, there was still a healthy mound of details that needed to be taken care of.

Therin dove right into the preparations and made himself available for all the press clamoring for information about the event. Big names in the political, sports and entertainment worlds were already making buzzes and offering their support to what many called the most enduring component of the nation's future: education.

The crazed workload was exactly what Therin needed. Leaving Kianti a week earlier had hit him harder than he'd expected. He felt as though some part of him had—and still was—shredded.

She'd asked no questions, only told him to handle the upset so they could pick up where they left off. Again, he weighed the very real obstacles of pursuing a relationship with her. If he'd planned on pulling away, the time to do so would have been right then. He was back in Vancouver; it'd be easy to break communication. A day could turn into a week, a week to a month... such thoughts, however, only angered him, making his already edgy mood razor-sharp.

Break communication—to not pursue her in every way imaginable was unfathomable to him. He wondered how deeply his feelings for her had gone. How *far would* they go?

The elevator doors opened before he could ponder an answer to the question. He approached the nurse's station and favored the three women standing there with one of his unconsciously devastating smiles. Of course, the smile was reciprocated and flavored with approving gazes as the women looked up at him.

Therin was told that Rick Dubose's condition had been upgraded. He could accept visitors and Therin was granted access. In a soft, appreciative manner he thanked the RNs but assured them that he didn't need a personal escort to the room.

Along the way, Therin's easy mood dimmed. His hands balled to fists inside the pockets of the quarter-length black denim jacket he wore. Rick could have been killed. He'd already experienced personal loss since the onset of his political career; could he afford to experience more?

Therin planted a quick knock to the tall oak door before cracking it open. Rick was sitting up in bed and frowning at the platter filled with what Therin suspected was food.

"Is it as good as it looks?" he queried with a grin.

Rick looked up and smiled before casting another skeptical look toward the tray. "I'm afraid it's *just* as good as it looks."

Laughter broke out between the two men. Soon though, Therin was bringing a hand down on Rick's shoulder.

"I'm sorry for what happened, man."

Rick tried to put on a happy face. "Thanks, but you can't be half as sorry as *I* am. I missed one helluva date."

Therin grinned. "May not be a total loss—she's probably very sympathetic to your injury."

Rick's glower seemed to fade. "You could have somethin' there…she did call and promise to smuggle me in a cheeseburger."

More laughter filled the room.

"I'm sorry that you got caught up in all this," Therin reiterated once the mood had sobered again.

"It's not your fault."

Therin removed his jacket. "From what I understand, it is."

Rick nodded. "You're talkin' about what the attacker said?"

"You remember anything else about him? Did he look familiar?"

"It's like I told the police. It was raining, he had on a top coat. A hat was covering half of his face." Rick smoothed hands across his shaved head. "Voice didn't sound familiar, either."

Aside from the low volume of commentary from the sportscasters on the overhead TV, the room was silent.

"I'll be damned," Rick breathed after a while.

Therin waited, watching as Rick winced while easing up higher on the bed.

"I didn't even think of it before," he whispered.

"What?" Therin inched closer on the chair he occupied near the bed. "You remember something else?"

"No." Rick was shaking his head. "Not exactly." He shrugged. "It's probably nothing. An assumption at best."

"Let's have it." Therin beckoned with a wave.

"Just somethin' about what he said."

"His voice?"

"No…His words—the words he used, to be exact."

Therin was quiet. He had no idea where Rick was headed with his train of thought.

"Sorry for being vague." A lopsided grin came to Rick's dark face. "Just before the guy stabbed me, he said, 'The boss is gonna get you all killed.'"

Therin bit his bottom lip and tried not to look too expectant. "Um…" He didn't want to make light of what seemed so important to the injured man, but he didn't get it.

Rick smiled as though he understood Therin's reaction. "I make my living writing speeches." He pressed a hand to the hospital gown where it covered his chest. "I'm apt to pay attention to how words are put together, which is often a more telling sign about people than they realize."

Therin leaned back on the chair. Folding arms across his chest, he settled in for the education.

"Saying something like, 'I hate what he stands for' is a far more telling statement than 'His interests are unpopular.'"

"Ah…" Therin stroked his jaw and nodded slow. "So something about what this guy said is gnawing at you?"

Rick worried the neckline of his gown. "I just wonder why he said '*the* boss' instead of '*your* boss.'" His expression was mildly guarded then. "It'd make sense that he wouldn't say '*our* boss,' he'd be announcing himself as—"

"Hold on." Therin bolted forward. "Are you thinking someone—someone on the staff could be responsible for this?"

Rick shook his head so rapidly that he cringed at the pain when it stirred near his wound. "It's probably nothin'. I only mentioned it because it struck me as strange that the jackass wouldn't say '*your* boss.'" He waved as if frustrated. "Like I *also* said, I write speeches for a living. Being anal about speech patterns is part of my job."

"Lie back, man." Therin moved the tray table back down the length of the bed. "Get your rest and lay off this a minute." He could see the conversation was taking its toll on the younger man.

"Probably just need a little sleep." Rick's eyelids were already lowering. "I don't think I'll be able…to let go of this…for a while."

Therin's smile was more of a grimace as he watched

Rick ease into sleep. He wholeheartedly agreed that *he* wouldn't let go of this for quite a while, either.

Neche, North Dakota~

Kianti wrapped herself more snuggly in the heavy baby blue sweater and admired the stock of supplies in her pantry. She selected a can of chunky vegetable soup from one of the shelves and went to heat it on the stove.

One day she was going to have to find a better way of thanking her neighbors Vernon and Wren Shay. The couple always included her pantry needs when they went to market. Autographed CDs and concert tickets seemed to pale in comparison to the very important service they provided without being asked. In a place like Neche, a simple dusting of snow could turn into a blizzard in no time flat.

Kianti set the soup on to simmer and took a look at the winter wonderland beyond the glass doors in the kitchen, which led out to the deck overlooking the rear of the property. She recalled when her father bought the place all those years ago. She and her mother thought he'd lost it. Now, Kianti couldn't think of another place she wanted to be when the pressures of her world got to be a little too much for her to handle.

Is that what happened in Cali? Had it all become too much to handle? She thought she'd behaved very maturely when he told her he suddenly had to go.

She'd been cool and unaffected enough when she told him they could pick up where they left off once he got back.

What else was she going to do? Tie him to her bed and make him stay? She smiled and went back to stir the soup while thinking what an enticing idea that was.

It was clear though that something had him on edge. She certainly hadn't wanted to leave him with the idea that she needed him to stay. Once he left, though, she found that the relaxation she often enjoyed in Pacifica wasn't working its usual magic. She headed north.

Brody and the guys were understandably concerned. They knew she only headed for the Dakotas when she was in need of complete seclusion. While the time away had its merits, a woman with her condition couldn't afford to be too cut off from the civilized world.

Regardless, her time there so far had been well spent. It kept the one week from feeling like three. She'd spent an ample amount of time finding out as much as she could about Therin Darius Rucker—only child of U.S. diplomat Farris Rucker and his wife, Denise. The couple had been killed in an automobile accident two years after Therin accepted the U.S. Ambassador's post. He resigned from the appointment three months later.

She'd studied every picture memorizing the lines and angles of his incredible face. In the midst of that, she wondered exactly when it was that she'd fallen in love with him.

Kianti shook off the silent admission and found a bowl for her soup. God, she hoped she'd done nothing to clue him in to that fact. She'd scare him away for sure.

But he hadn't been scared yet, she pondered, spoon poised over the pot. He'd actually surprised her by how well he'd dealt with what she'd told him about her health. Even so, she'd been waiting for the other shoe to drop wondering when it would all become too much for him to handle.

She settled down to the gold tweed sofa in the mini living area in a far corner of the kitchen. She warmed her hands around the soup bowl and inhaled its aroma when she blew softly across the surface.

It's been over a week and he hasn't called your cell once. It took effort to swallow the soup then with that in mind. If he didn't call by week's end, would she do the deed? After all, hadn't she boasted about being a woman who didn't beat around the bush when it came to getting what she wanted?

Focused on that line of thought, she was halfway through her soup when a sound thundered somewhere in the distance.

"Jeez!" she hissed, and her heart lurched painfully as her hands tightened on the bowl. Gradually, she acknowledged that the sound radiated from the front. She took her time in making her way to answer and received another shock when she pulled open the door.

Therin bounded inside, not stopping until he'd gathered her tight against the silver-toned bomber jacket he wore.

Kianti only shivered a moment next to the jacket slick with melting snow. "Therin—"

He pulled away suddenly and gave her a tiny jerk. "What are you doing? What the hell did you think you were doing scaring me that way?" His face was dark with anger and a fair amount of concern.

"Scaring *you?*" she whispered only to have him tug her close again.

"Don't ever do that to me again." The command was muffled as his face was hidden in her neck.

He was kissing her before she could say anything and Kianti forgot all else. He lifted her higher against him, kicking the heavy door shut and carrying her into the house.

Chapter 11

A series of hushed directions whispered against Therin's shoulder led him to Kianti's bedroom.

"How'd you find me?" she asked once he'd set her to her feet and proceeded to undress her.

"Casey told me after I went to your place and found you gone," he grumbled while tugging the sweater from her shoulders. A sunflower-yellow tank top followed.

"Why didn't you try my cell?" She shivered as more of her body was bared to his sights and touch.

"Wanted to surprise you." He squeezed her calf, silently urging her from the sweats and panties he'd tugged down to her feet. "Wasn't until I came all the way out here that I got pissed as hell."

"Why?" she whispered even as he lifted her bare form and settled her to the middle of the bed.

"What are you doing all the way out here in the

middle of nowhere with a snowstorm barreling down on you?"

"I..." Kianti found she couldn't lock in on the words she needed. She could only stare in awe as he stood over her, rugged and pissed off while shrugging out of his boots, jacket and toboggan.

"I have neighbors." The words were slow in coming. She wanted to moan instead when he tugged the sweater over his head to reveal his muscle-cut abdomen. He was half-undressed, garbed only in the dark low-rise jeans.

Kianti left her explanations and snuggled into him when he covered her on the bed. She shivered anew at the sensation of his toned chest against her. The friction of the rough denim next to her bare thighs only enhanced her pleasure.

Their kissing resumed deep and heated. Therin cupped her neck in his hand to hold her still while he rotated his tongue around hers. She locked her legs high about his back and ground down on the delicious bulge straining behind the zipper of his jeans. Tingles riddled her body, but she reached down to help him out of the confinements.

Therin refused her assistance, preferring to drive her insane with his hands and mouth. He left no part of her untouched, raking his nose over and under her breasts. He paid extra attention to the dark firm nipples and inhaled her scent when his nose dipped into her belly-button. When she'd orgasmed twice, and believed she could stand no more, he proved her wrong.

Jerkily, he came out of the denims, grabbing a pack of condoms from one of the back pockets before he cast them aside.

Therin pressed a packet into her palm and indulged in more kissing and caressing.

It was no easy task, considering his every brush to her skin had her aching and moaning open-mouthed into the air. She emerged victorious, however. Once protection was in its place, she guided him inside her. A trembling sound filtered past her lips when he thrust long and deep.

No thoughts of going slow occurred to either of them. The room was illuminated by the falling snow and by the robust sounds of their impassioned voices.

"This is incredible." Therin admitted to the beauty beyond the tall paned windows in Kianti's bedroom. It was much later and they lay cuddled there watching the snow continue its descent. His arms tightened about her and he hid his face in her hair to inhale the fragrance.

"I don't see how they can leave you out here alone, though," he murmured.

"Remember the neighbors I told you about?" Kianti's voice sounded slow and sleepy as she savored her contentment. "It was the only way I could convince the guys to give me time out here."

"Still…"

"Therin, I'm pretty sure the guys have already been aggravating Wren and Vern like crazy—asking if they can see any lights burning over here and crap like that."

Therin couldn't help but give in to laughter.

"I don't know what all they can see two miles up the road anyway but…" She yawned.

"Two miles." Therin tensed.

"They're the best neighbors anyone could ask for."

She nudged his abs with her elbow and smiled. "Wren's a nurse and Vern's a veterinarian. I'd say that covers me on the healthcare end, wouldn't you?"

He gathered her closer. "What do you do out here?" His voice vibrated against the back of her neck.

She laughed. "Therin, I'm not on the moon! We do the same things as everyone else—shopping, movies… We just have to travel a bit farther to do it. Chicago's not far, then there's Winnipeg."

"Guess I never thought there were black people in North Dakota—or South, for that matter."

"We're very, *very* few and far between. Closest I've come to finding another person of color is Wren. She's Native American—Chippewa."

"And Vern the vet?" Therin teased, grunting playfully when her elbow poked him again.

"He's a regular white guy and they're two of my best friends."

"I'd like to meet them." He felt her cringe. "What?"

"Just that you being here won't be a secret for long if they find out, and once the guys call…"

"You want us to be a secret?" His light eyes narrowed.

She sighed, turning her face into a pillow. "There's little I can claim for my own, you know? A private life is one of those things. Even if it's only a few stolen moments, I'll take 'em."

Therin kissed her cheek. "I can accept that, 'specially if it gives me more time to have you to myself."

A naughty smile curved her mouth as she bumped her bottom against his firming sex. "And what will you do with me now that you've got me all to yourself?"

Wild laughter flew from her throat when he flipped her to her back.

"Shall I tell you or show you?"

"Both," she gasped, and giggled only a moment before his kiss silenced her.

Therin pushed up amidst the covers. He frowned into the darkened room while rubbing fingers through the wavy hair covering his head. He didn't bother calling out for Kianti. He already sensed she wasn't there next to him in the huge bed. Pushing back the covers, he left the bed and padded naked through the dark silence.

He heard her breathing when he stepped into the den. Her wheezing caught his ears. She was lying on the sofa covered by an afghan. A kiss pressed to her temple told him she was shivering. Something told Therin that it wasn't because she was cold.

Without hesitation, he checked her pulse and hissed an obscenity. Bounding from the den, he returned less than a minute later with a glass of water...and a pill. Gently, he eased her into a sitting position.

"Take it." He pressed the medication to her palm.

"No." She grimaced weakly and tried to push it back to him. "Therin, no..." She made a pitiful attempt at twisting out of his embrace.

"Take it on your own or I put it down your throat myself." His voice was sweet but no less firm.

"Damn you." She coughed and closed her eyes. "Do you know how long I've gone without—?"

"Forget it."

When she opened her eyes, they were swimming in tears.

Therin braced one hand to the arm of the sofa and the other along the back, effectively trapping her. "Forget it." He persisted.

Kianti threw the pill into her mouth and glared defiantly as she swallowed. She would have settled back to the sofa, but Therin took her up in his arms. He put her back to bed, but didn't join her. He watched her until she drifted back into sleep.

Late the next morning, Kianti walked into the kitchen wearing a foul expression that grew fouler when she spotted Therin enjoying coffee in the mini living area.

"Feeling better?" he asked, his gaze hooded as it raked her from head to toe.

"You don't know what you've done." Her voice came out as a hiss.

Therin shrugged. "I thought I understood Brody's instructions pretty well." He blew across the surface of the creamy coffee. "Oh, he gave me a new bottle of your prescription," Therin explained when he saw her mouth fall open at his mention of Brody's name. "He figured you wouldn't tell me where to find them if it turned out you'd need them…"

"Sons of bitches," she murmured, raking all ten fingers through her hair. "Who the hell do you think you are?"

"The man sharing your bed," he spoke without hesitation.

"That doesn't give you the right—"

"It gives me every right."

She rolled her eyes and sauntered toward the kitchen.

"Don't flatter yourself, Therin. I've got four like you back home. I'm not in the mood to collect another."

He bolted to his feet and caught her halfway across the kitchen. "You don't have *any* like me."

She blinked, the nasty flip mood that'd been building depleted like a popped balloon. She knew further arguments would be unwise. Besides, he was right. She didn't have any like him. She never had.

"Go back to bed." He brushed past her. "I'll bring your breakfast and wake you in time for dinner with the Shays. Yeah, I've already met them." He went to collect his coffee cup and didn't bother to turn and witness her stunned expression. "Wren already rushed home to make a pot of her special stew. We can make your last night here a memorable one—nicely memorable, that is."

"Last night?" She watched him calmly rubbing a hand across his carved abs as he drained his coffee cup.

"We're going to Canada in the morning."

"Canada? But I can't just—"

"Already forgotten your commitment to my event, I guess?" He propped a hand to the waistband of his sleep pants and waited.

Kianti opened her mouth and then closed it.

"Right." He strolled into the kitchen to start her breakfast. "Besides, you're out of your mind if you think I'll leave you alone here after—" He stopped himself, not wanting to remember the fear that had gripped him the night before. "Go to bed, Kia," he ordered in the softest tone he could muster.

* * *

Vernon and Wren Shay's home was the epitome of Southwestern motif. The beauty of Wren's previous native Arizona life was apparent in every room of the house in such a way that the warmth of the area radiated from every space.

The two couples enjoyed hot cocoa and coffee from the deck overlooking the Western portion of the expansive property. From there, the group had an unforgettable view of the setting sun at the snowy horizon. The abundance of conversation settled as well. The foursome soaked in the late-afternoon coziness, which was enhanced by the fragrance of the simmering stew and baking bread from indoors.

Therin appreciated solitude as much as anyone but couldn't for the life of him understand how two city kids could make a life where the market was fifteen miles away.

"Sounds crazy, we know," Vernon said when the high volume of laughter lowered a few decibels. "But you know things can happen in a person's life that make one decision appear like the only sane choice." He settled down deeper into the cushioned wood chair he occupied and smiled as a quick chilly wind ruffled his thick brown hair.

"I can't speak for Wren—" he gave his wife an adoring wink "—but being out here for the past ten of our sixteen years of marriage, I've never felt more able to think and to feel like my thoughts have a clarity." He warmed his hands about a mug of black coffee and shrugged. "Now, one could argue that those thoughts were there even when we lived in L.A., but I'll be damned if I could find 'em."

"I'm guessing Therin can relate to us on that, hon." Wren spoke to her husband but her wide dark stare was trained on Therin. "There's a solitary beauty to Vancouver. Sure, it's a bit more…busy than the Dakotas, but it's similar."

Therin was already nodding. His light eyes slid from Wren's face to the unending view. "There've definitely been times in my life when that solitude was what I needed."

Kianti had been relatively silent while nursing her cocoa. She studied Therin closely, wondering at what he was thinking of. What had those *times* in his life entailed? She didn't have long to wonder, for soon Vernon was probing a bit deeper into Therin's response.

"I guess an ambassador's life isn't all fancy parties and glamour, huh?"

Therin laughed, stroking his index finger along a sideburn as he sobered. "Those fancy parties and glamour have their price, man. There're a lot of sacrifices I had to make during the course of my post." He frowned a little then. "I guess if I hadn't taken my duty so seriously, the sacrifices may not have been so costly." Again, he laughed and put a rather sheepish smile in place.

"Now that I've put a cloud over the evening…"

The Shays joined Therin in hearty laughter.

"Well, you know out here we're used to clouds," Vern said and leaned over to clink his coffee mug against Therin's.

New discussion began. Kianti maintained her quiet, preferring to spend her time studying Therin.

Chapter 12

The trip to Vancouver from Neche wasn't a straight shot. Therin wanted to take his time with the trip. Instead of calling for the plane that brought him to Kianti in North Dakota, he decided on driving part of the way.

They took advantage of that, making frequent stops along the way. There was the International Peace Garden in Manitoba, Canada. Unfortunately, because of the time of year, it was impossible to take a look at the Floral Clock. Still, the time was well spent and the couple enjoyed sharing stories of their past visits to the incredible site.

Later, there was lunch at a greasy spoon café that they both adored. Conversation revolved around Therin's high-powered friends and Kianti's fans—what would those folks think if they saw them there?

Despite the informality of the day, Kianti felt a bit taken aback. She grew more silent the closer they came to Vancouver. Therin was being recognized a bit more frequently by then. This posed no problem. Kianti was captivated by the ease with which he greeted the average joes who wanted to talk politics or even hockey. He possessed a definite charm that wasn't some trick that he'd picked up from the campaign trails he'd traveled as a politician. His charm was natural and easy. Kianti could almost feel it and she relished the warmth.

Kianti's observance of Therin switched to an even higher gear with they arrived at the penthouse apartment he kept at a Vancouver hotel.

Royalty indeed, she thought while taking in all the attention paid to the unassuming thirty-something black man with looks to die for and charm to spare. In spite of what she already knew about him, she kept expecting his demeanor to change. She looked for him to grow cocky or arrogant because of all the elaborate bowing and scraping he received. Nothing changed, though. He never changed. Kianti found herself more enchanted by him because of it.

Sadly though, at least as far as Kianti saw it, reality set in like dead weight. It was early evening when they arrived at the golden-lit, elegant living quarters he kept on the top floor along with a suite of offices.

Shortly however, the bellmen and hotel concierge left them alone. Kianti discovered Therin's opinions about her healthcare were also unchanged.

"That's right…mmm-hmm…baked Mahi, rolls and steamed veggies." Therin looked over at Kianti, brows raised for her approval of the meal he called down for.

When she gave him the thumbs-up, he winked. "Sounds good…all right, thanks."

"Do you want your pill before or after you eat?" He set the cordless back to the charging dock and shot her a quick glance over his shoulder.

Kianti felt her heart sink but braced back her disappointment. "Neither," she stubbornly replied.

"All right." Therin shrugged, pulling off the black fleece hoody he wore over a simple white T-shirt. "Before, then," he decided.

She rolled her eyes. "Therin, don't do this. Please. Not when we've had such a great time."

"You're right." He walked toward her, not stopping until he was bracing hands on the back of the sofa. "We have had a great time. I intend on us having a great night, too."

Kianti wouldn't let herself be swayed by his meaning. She held on to her stubbornness.

"Don't think that my…episode the other night means I'm ready to start a new regimen with those things."

Therin bowed his head, feeling his jaw muscles tighten in tandem with the rising of his temper. A smile cut through the frustration. She had the ability to rile him so easily and he continued to be amazed by it.

"Those *things* help keep you alive. You do realize that, don't you?"

She brought a fist down to the back of the sofa. "You're letting Brody set you on edge with that overprotective streak of his."

Therin's bright deep-set gaze registered disbelief. "How can such a gifted woman be so dense? So obtuse about her own life?"

Kianti leaned back on the sofa and began to chew on her thumbnail. "You can't understand this."

Therin muttered a curse and paced behind the sofa.

"You don't know how it feels to grow up different because you can play Beethoven at six and then even more different because you've got the heart of someone three times your age. To hell with it." The flared sleeves of her sweater whipped wildly when she waved him off. "Nothing's worth being tied to those things a minute longer than I have to be." She raised her chin defiantly.

"That may be dense and obtuse but it's *my* choice and I have no intention to go back on it." Something flickered in her dark, tilting stare. "Not even for the promise of enjoying a fully charged love scene with you."

Therin stopped pacing then and rounded the sofa where she reclined. "You think that's why I'm doing this?" He brought his hands down on either side of her when she tried to move. "You think I'm more concerned with not being pestered by the possibility of you dying on me?"

She lowered her head, instantly regretting her words.

"Second bedroom on the other side of the living room," he grumbled and left the sofa. "You'll find your things already there. Dinner should be up in twenty." He left the room without a look back.

Kianti stayed behind. She left the sofa and made a slow trek across the living room to take in the view of the city from the floor-to-ceiling windows that lined the entire wall. She was contented by the late-evening view of lights just beginning to twinkle against the bluish-purple sky. She removed the pill bottle from the front pocket of her jeans.

Smiling then, she thought of her four—*five* protectors. She wondered if they'd believe that she had never kept the bottle too far. She thought back to what she'd just said to Therin.

Nothing could make her change her mind about taking them. That wasn't true. That was so very far from the truth.

"Can't tell you how happy I am to have you around to help me plan this thing." Therin chuckled over something Ruby had just said. "I still wish you'd taken more time off, though. If anybody deserves it, it's you."

"I'm much better off at work, Therin." Ruby sighed over the line. "All that time off and I'm liable to get into more trouble."

"Well, the offer still stands if you change your mind about taking more time."

"Thanks, Therin. Listen, I'll call when I have more info about those lighting crews."

"Sounds good." A soft knock fell to Therin's bedroom door when he set down the phone. "It's open," he called.

Kianti ventured no farther than the doorway. "Dinner's here."

He nodded, taking in the length of her before leaving the armchair. "I'll be out in a sec. You don't have to wait for me."

Kianti turned to leave the room but changed her mind. "Therin? I'm sorry for what I let you think…I know you said it because you care."

Therin nodded even while the voice inside his head demanded that he tell her the truth. In the short while he'd known her, during the few stolen moments they'd shared, he'd fallen in love with her.

Kianti didn't know what to make of his silence, so she nodded and turned again to give him his privacy.

"Um…" He waited for her to turn again. "There's a piano down in one of the lounges. The desk knows you want to practice, so they've sectioned it off. No one should disturb you there."

Her smile wavered. "Thanks."

Stares lingered for a time before they parted ways.

Dinner was a *strained* quiet affair. The Mahi and vegetables were perfectly cooked and seasoned. However, the effects of the lengthy trip finally began to grate at them once they'd had the chance to wind down. Silent decisions had been made on both sides—to call it a night following the delicious meal.

Kianti offered no argument when Therin leaned over to set a pill to the edge of her saucer. She took it without argument, too plain tuckered out to make an issue of it. The doorbell buzzed and they each gave a start at the interruption.

"I'll go." She dabbed a linen napkin to her mouth.

"What for?" Therin queried around a bit of Mahi.

"You've got business."

"Ah." He waved off her reasoning and pushed back from the table. "My staff needs to see that I haven't been lying about you." He was on his way to the double gold-trimmed maplewood doors.

"Aside from Vaughn, none of them believe I know you, let alone have a relationship with you."

Kianti blinked at his words and would have appreciated hearing more on their "relationship."

The bell sounded again, though, just as Therin turned the lever. Vaughn Burgess entered along with Gary Bryce and Peter Stanson. The group arrived with hearty greetings and handshakes. They quieted and grew downright subdued when they spotted the petite cinnamon-brown beauty at the table across the living room.

"Kianti Lawrence. Gary Bryce and Peter Stanson." Therin grinned, taking great enjoyment in their awe.

Vaughn gave each man a nudge when they simply stood there gawking. Gary and Peter finally stepped forward to shake hands with Kianti.

"It's nice to see you again, Ms. Lawrence," Vaughn said, offering his hand next.

"My wife and I really enjoy your work," Peter said once he'd regained his verbal abilities.

"Thank you so much. I hope I'll have the chance to meet her during Therin's event."

"We're honored to have you be a part of this," Vaughn said.

"I'm the one who's honored." Kianti smiled and then clasped her hands together. "Well, guys, that trip really wiped me out. I think I'm gonna go turn in. Good night."

There was another round of handshakes and lingering looks toward Therin before she left the room.

Still grinning over his associates' reactions, Therin

smoothed a hand across the front of his T-shirt and resumed his place at the table to finish the last of his Mahi.

"Jesus, Ther." Gary was still looking in the direction Kianti had exited. "Vaughn must be some kind of talker to convince you to leave her in California."

Therin grinned. "It wasn't easy."

"She's so little," Peter noted.

"Hmph." Therin drained his bottle of Sam Adams. "Don't let that fool you. She's a tough one."

"Sorry for bothering you here your first night back, man."

Therin shrugged toward Vaughn. "Anything wrong?"

"Nah, nothing like that." Vaughn took a seat at Kianti's place. "Everything's on schedule. The first members of the organization are arriving and have already checked into their rooms."

"Bose Cooper and Marley Terrio asked about getting together for breakfast in the morning," Peter said.

Therin nodded. "Not a problem."

Vaughn smirked. "You sure?" He was envisioning the two very revered, very outspoken senior members of the EYES organization.

Peter and Gary chuckled, but Therin wasn't offended.

"Tell 'em I'll be there," Therin confirmed with a grin before he sobered. "So talk to me about Rick, how's he doin'?"

"They released him from the hospital while you were in North Dakota," Gary said.

"Does he remember anything more about what the guy said?"

Vaughn, Peter and Gary exchanged looks and then asked their boss for clarification. The three listened while Therin told them about Rick's interpretation of the attacker's words.

"Did he recognize the voice?" Gary asked.

"How can he accuse a member of the staff and he can't even lock in on the voice," Peter argued.

"Hold up, guys." Vaughn raised his hands. "Rick didn't actually accuse anybody. He's only questioning the way the guy phrased his words, right, Ther?"

Therin smiled in confirmation. "I know it sounds weird, but there's a reason Rick's so good at what he does. If he feels there's something to this, we'd be fools not to take it seriously."

Therin massaged his eyes and set aside the file he really hadn't been reading. He only wanted to check on Kianti. She'd been so drained when she turned in a few hours ago… He only wanted to be sure she was okay.

Sounds good, Ther. He convinced himself when in reality his motives were far less noble. Shutting off the lamp in his study, he set out for the room on the other side of the living room.

Kianti hadn't locked the door and he hesitated before twisting the knob. For a time, he stood watching her from the doorway. She didn't stir and, after a while, he moved farther inside the room.

She was a rough sleeper, he mused. Shapely limbs peeked out from a disarray of pillows and covers. His fingertips tingled, aching to touch her.

Lightly, he trailed the back of his hand across her calf and then dutifully eased the covers back into place.

Kianti stirred, murmuring something incoherent. Therin took a seat on the edge of the bed and brushed coarse smoky black tufts of hair away from her face. The innocent touch quickly grew bolder and he clenched a fist when he realized that. He was cursing himself for taking the least bit of advantage of her, when he felt her hands clutching his. She drew it down to the sheets, beneath them…

"Kia…you need your rest…"

"Please…just a little, mmm…"

It was his undoing. Kianti bit her lip when she got what she craved and felt his fingers at work inside her.

"Therin, no…" she moaned when he stopped.

The disappointment didn't last long. Therin was kissing her deeply and she reciprocated. The session was heated and unrestrained as tensions were set free. Kianti sought a measure of control as usual and, *as usual,* Therin denied her.

There was no disappointment, however, in the love they made. They were both equally aroused, equally pleasured. Therin could scarcely control himself, he needed her so.

"Let go.…" she urged, not seeming to mind his prowess.

Therin knew it was up to him to exercise caution. Next to impossible against her whispered commands for him to take her the way he wanted.

Chapter 13

Kianti woke early and headed down to the reserved lounge for practice the next morning. While the hotel staff barred guests from intruding on the artist's rehearsal time, the rule obviously didn't apply to them.

Remote seats in the sultry dim elegance of the lounge had already been selected. Various members of the staff indulged in an early-morning treat of exquisite playing.

The audience included Therin. He woke frowning when he realized Kianti wasn't there next to him. She did, however, leave a brief note on her pillow. The way she began the message said so much about them.

Don't worry...

Would it always be his first emotion where it related to her? Concern? In the relaxing environment of the lounge, he contemplated as he watched her behind the mammoth-size piano.

The group was mesmerized by her performance—not

only by the playing but by the look of the musician herself. Therin kept his expression passive, but adored the way Kianti's body swayed and dipped to the haunting harmony.

Concern. The emotion had certainly played a role within him the night before. In truth, concern played a role every night he had her.

Let go, she urged throughout their lovemaking.

Her power over his emotions would have him doing just that and very soon. His mouth set into a grim line then. He didn't want to lose her, not when he'd never dared to imagine she existed. Life was such a fragile thing. He'd learned that the hard way. It was too fragile to risk for something as fleeting as pleasure....

Applause drew him gently from his thoughts. He joined in only briefly and left the lounge without being noticed.

Bose Cooper and Marley Terrio were the two retired university presidents who had been instrumental in bringing Therin aboard the EYES project. When they'd requested the breakfast meeting, Therin hadn't thought of refusing. The three were so often busy they rarely had time for phone chats, let alone meals together.

Therin arrived at the private restaurant, La Olivete, quite pleased by the opportunity to meet with his old acquaintances.

"How's that staff of yours hanging in these days?" Marley Terrio inquired.

Therin's jaw tightened. It didn't take more than that seemingly innocent inquiry to tell him the men had been experiencing similar difficulties.

Bose chuckled. "Did you think you were the only one, son?"

"Considering all the shit that's come down on me since I hung my hat in the political ring...yes. I guess you could say I did." Therin leaned forward to massage his neck below the collar of his crisp shirt.

Bose and Marley nodded their understanding of the misfortunes the younger man had spoken of.

"I've let all but two of my staff go," Marley said, once he and his colleague shared with Therin all the *incidents* that had befallen various members of their staff.

"Like you, we were hoping to give the bastards a clear shot at us," Bose added.

Therin grinned. "Vaughn told me I was a fool to think it'd work."

The two men laughed.

"I've got a feeling the opposition would rather come at us on a more public stage," Marley said.

"Are you thinking they might try something this weekend?" Therin hesitated on drinking from his coffee mug. "It'd be the perfect opportunity. Hell." He rubbed a hand across his hair. "Should I be calling off the general's announcement?"

Again, Marley and Bose shared a chuckle over their young friend's expense.

"Shep Yale wouldn't give the jackasses the satisfaction of not using the opportunity to stick it to 'em," Bose declared.

"We should at least let them know of our concerns," Therin cautioned.

"Just don't expect him to back down." Marley added an obscene amount of sugar to his black coffee. "He's got a point to prove and when you reach our age, proving points are worth the sacrifices."

Therin winced over the use of Marley's final word. He leaned across the table to shake hands with both men.

Therin and Kianti were leaving the hotel by lunchtime and headed for his home just outside Vancouver. Conversation flowed easily between them during the chauffeured ride, but silenced altogether on Kianti's part when she saw the house beyond the towering brass gates.

"It won't bite you," Therin teased from his reclining position across the long backseat. Her uncertainty was easy to spot.

"The way you live…" she breathed, thinking of the condo, the bowing and scraping she'd witnessed during the past several days and now this. "This place is unreal."

Therin smoothed his thumb across a brow. "This from a woman who keeps a fortress in Pacifica."

She looked back at him from the window. "Touché." The house drew closer and she smiled. "You have to admit, though…I'll bet you couldn't get around to visiting all the rooms in this place in a year."

"Hey! The rooms aren't *that* big."

"Mmm-hmm." Her response to his wounded cry was laced with doubt.

"Thanks, Ed," Therin called toward the front of the car when the driver pulled to a stop. "I got her," he said before leaving the car to assist Kianti from her side.

"They're only here for the event," Therin said when

he treated Kianti to an impromptu tour and introduced her to the house staff.

Kianti bit her lip on a grin as they walked a long bright corridor. "What? You don't think I'd approve otherwise?"

"I wouldn't."

"Goes against your principles?"

Therin eased his hands into his khaki pockets and shrugged.

When they got to the ballroom, where the piano performance would take place, Kianti lost her breath. It was a magnificent space of chandeliers, round glass tables and tall windows with alluring views of the grounds. The piano occupied a corner of the large square oak dance floor. Kianti walked around the room as though she were in a daze. She observed the skylights surrounding the chandeliers and could imagine the effect of the golden light mingled with starlight.

"Can't believe all this is for me."

Therin laughed and strolled the long edge of the floor. "What I can't believe is that you're so surprised by all this when you've probably played in halls four times as big as this ballroom."

"But this is a home." She trailed her fingers across the cushiony, amber suede sofas and oversize armchairs situated behind the round tables. "This is a home," she repeated.

In that moment, Therin didn't know if he'd ever had such enjoyment in that room.

"You should check out that piano." He spoke in a hasty manner when she noticed him staring.

"I'm sure it's fine," she whispered, passing the

instrument without a look as she moved closer to Therin. She brought her hands to his biceps and then stood on her toes to kiss his cheek. "Thank you."

"Thank *me?* It's *you* who's doing me this favor."

Kianti shrugged toying with the zipper tab of his blue-gray pullover. "You've just shown me how much you appreciate it."

Before she could set down on her feet, he gathered her tight and plied her with a deeper kiss. Kianti moved forward, nudging him until he was seated on the back of one of the armchairs. She stepped between his thighs and became a more eager participant in the kiss. She tugged his hand to the front of her blouse and arched her breast against his palm.

A clearing throat drew them apart moments later. Therin pressed his forehead to hers and inhaled for a few additional seconds before he looked toward the door.

"Sorry for interrupting."

"Come over here," Therin waved, taking Kianti along with him as they headed for the front of the room. "Kianti Lawrence, I'd like you to meet Morgan Felts, my chief of security," he said, watching as Morgan behaved in the same awed manner his associates had when they first met Kianti.

"It's a pleasure, Ms. Lawrence."

"Please call me Kianti." She shook Morgan's hand and then glanced quickly across her shoulder. "I should go check out that piano so...it was nice meeting you, Morgan. Hope to see you at the event."

Therin allowed Morgan a few more seconds to ogle. "So what's up?" He clapped the man's shoulder.

"Rick." Morgan cleared his throat. "The guys said he had some ideas about what the attacker told him."

"Has anyone been acting strange around the office?" Therin asked once he'd recapped Rick Dubose's theory.

Morgan only shook his head.

Therin noticed him grimace. "What?"

"Everybody's edgy as hell around the office." Morgan raked back the thick blondish-brown tufts of his hair. "Rick's probably grasping at straws here hoping to come up with something that'll put everyone else at ease."

Therin reclaimed his spot on the back of the chair and watched Morgan pace. "So you think there's nothing to this?"

"That's exactly what I think, and the folks who attacked Rick were most likely counting on you to make somethin' of it." Morgan punched a fist to one of the sofa pillows. "Hell, Therin, they know what the guy does for a living—it's probably why he was targeted in the first place."

Contemplating the theory, Therin moved the back of his hand along a sideburn. "Thanks, Morgan." He saw the man's expectant stare and nodded. "Will we see you tomorrow night?"

At ease then, Morgan grinned. "You're crazy if you think I'd miss out on a free concert by Kianti Lawrence."

"How often do you get to enjoy this?"

Kianti and Therin took in the sunset from the roof of his home. The construction from that end of the house was designed flat to accommodate the coffee table and stuffed lounge chairs. The area was treated for the abundance of snow that fell during the year and could become a weight issue for a flat roof.

Therin kept Kianti snuggled into his lap. "I almost never get to enjoy it." He kept his chin propped to her shoulder. "I just had it checked out for the event this weekend. Hope it'll go over well with the guests."

"Oh, I'm sure it will." She shrugged. "Speaking as a guest and all."

Therin kissed her cheek. "Does it make you want to give a big donation to my organization?"

Kianti turned so that she was straddling him. "The organization will definitely get a big donation." She settled down snug on top of him. "I've got something else in mind for its spokesman."

A kiss ensued, growing hot in an instant. As they were alone, Therin didn't think twice about baring her to his gaze and to his mouth.

"Don't stop," she begged when his mouth closed over the nipple he'd bared. "Mmm…" She thrust herself against his tongue while grinding more insistently against his lap.

"Damn." His hands flexed about her thighs and he stood to take her with him. "I really wanted you to see that sunset," he growled and carried her inside for what he wanted more.

The EYES Fundraiser and Membership Drive was set to be an important event as well as a glamorous one. Therin's elaborate home would be the site of the event as well as lodging for various members during the weekend.

Though the gathering was for a serious cause, much of the buzz surrounded the entertainment the ex-ambassador had pulled together. Such an accomplishment was further proof that the man carried friends in more lucrative areas than politics.

Kianti's name surged among the buzz, yet she found herself just as starstruck as anyone. On hand for the affair were two hip-hop moguls she'd been dying to meet. Upon meeting Kianti, however, the gentlemen were interested in beginning talks on a possible collaborative effort with her and few of their artists.

Therin kept Kianti on his arm quite frequently. He introduced her to the rest of his staff and other members of the organization. They were near the piano talking with Peter Stanson and his wife, Chloe, when several guests moved in to ask if Kianti was about to grace them with a performance. The lovely pianist graciously obliged. The room silenced, making way for the mesmerizing piece she performed.

Later, Therin and Kianti shared a dance in the center of the candlelit dance floor. They barely swayed to the exotic melody looming about and simply treasured the closeness. Therin kept his face hidden in her neck bared by her upswept hair. He inhaled the light appealing fragrance of her perfume and sighed. Many times, his arms flexed about her minute frame as though he were proving to himself that she was actually there next to him. Kianti was lost in the embrace as well. Therin was stroking her bare skin visible by the design of the airy black dress that flared playfully at her knees. The dress was both elegant and provocative with its plunging

V-neck and open back. Therin toyed with the triple set of gold O-rings securing the wide straps that joined at the small of her back.

The couple was oblivious to all the whispers and notice they received. There was no question that they were an "item" and also no question that the involvement was anything but shallow.

"You know…" Kianti blinked and scanned the room they twirled around in. "I don't think I've seen this room before."

Reluctantly, Therin raised his head from her shoulder. "It's good to have a place where the guests can retreat." He graced her with a sly wink. "This room…is off-limits to the press."

"Mmm…no press, huh? I like it." She gave a playful tug to his bowtie. "Well, if you're hoping to keep us a secret, I don't think you've done too good a job."

Therin's expression sobered. "I'm not trying to do a good job of that. I want everyone to know you're mine."

Kianti reconsidered her rebuttal and pressed her lips together.

"What?" He dipped his head to focus in on her more closely. "What?"

It was too late for silence, she realized. She could see the temper stirring in his brilliant stare. "How far are you expecting all this to go between us?" she whispered. She held on to her courage when he bristled. "I just can't help but point out *again* our lifestyles—very different—very hectic and very distant… Then there's the issue of my health, I—" She gasped when his hold tightened suddenly at her waist. "Therin—"

"Maybe I should be asking what *you* expect to come from all this between us?"

She'd always celebrated her ability to say what she wanted. No coy games… Now, she couldn't live up to that ability. The thought of telling him she loved him and wanted him with her always was too frightening.

If only he'd say it first…which was what she hoped for. That'd give her the courage to share her thoughts… maybe.

Again, she bowed her head so he couldn't see her rolling her eyes as she cursed the idiocy of that. She was saved, though, when they were interrupted a few seconds later.

"Mr. Ambassador? It's time."

"Thanks, Owen." Therin smiled over at the young man who'd touched his shoulder. He looked back down at Kianti, apology filling his gaze when he smiled.

"You've got to go to work," she said before he could speak a word.

"I want us to finish this." He linked his fingers through one of the dress rings to keep her still.

"We will." She patted his chest reassuringly. "There'll be time."

He searched her deep dark gaze for a lengthy moment and then kissed her forehead hard and offered an arm. Together, they left the dance floor.

Chapter 14

Therin and Kianti parted ways shortly after they returned to the main ballroom. Moments after their presence was discovered, they were drawn apart by various guests including Kianti's crew, who had just arrived shortly before the second hour of the event.

She left Therin talking with a few of his guests, while the guys escorted her to the table she'd had reserved for them.

"Thank you so much for coming," she said while making the rounds once the men had taken their seats. She pressed loud kisses to their cheeks.

"And thank *you* for scoring us an invite to this thing," Cube said. His mouth was full of canapés from the extensive buffet table.

Kianti waved a hand. "I couldn't pass up a chance like this to impress the hell out of you."

"Well, you did the hell out of that," Winton said.

"I'm not the only one." She took her place at the table and regarded them each with warm smiles. "You guys have impressed me, too. Entrusting me to the care of a man you don't really know."

"We know enough." Winton poured his Red Stripe into a chilled mug. "Therin seems like a good guy."

Kianti's rich laughter mirrored the vibrancy in her dark eyes. "You're only saying that because he's an ambassador."

"Ex," Khan corrected while flashing her a critical look. "You really shouldn't get so caught up over titles, Key."

Kianti replied by sticking out her tongue.

"It's obvious the guy cares about you, girl." Brody brought a measure of seriousness to the discussion with his observation.

"Crystal clear," Cube said around another mouthful of the canapés.

"Still gonna be tough making this work." Kianti sighed, propping her chin to her palm.

"That's why we took a step back." Winton shrugged. "Give you two the chance to see that. But I'm guessing it doesn't matter much since you guys are still together and lookin' all crazy in love."

A horrified look crept to Kianti's face. "In love?" she blurted.

Khan rolled his eyes. "Don't even try it, Key."

"Please don't," Winton added. "'Cause you ain't foolin' a soul with that confusion crap."

"I know, right?" Cube was wiping his hands then. "You look at the guy like he's drippin' in diamonds and he acts like you're the only woman he can see."

"What do any of you know about lookin' at a woman like she's the *only* woman?" Kianti tried to tease in an effort not to become too heady over the remarks.

The guys pretended to be offended. "We've all loved and lost, Kianti," Winton shared.

She grinned. "Mmm-hmm. I can definitely believe the 'lost' part."

"Seriously, Key." Cube reached for her hand and smothered it within his own. "We all know what being in love looks like and that dude looks as elated and tortured as anyone we've ever seen. Love's the only reason."

Kianti brought her hand down over Cube's. "He hasn't said anything about it—about…love."

"Have you?" Brody asked.

She frowned. "Well, I can't say it before he does."

The men burst into laughter.

"Typical!" Khan and Cube bellowed in unison.

"We'd have expected more of you, Key." Winton laughed and used Cube's napkin to wipe a tear from his eye.

"Why are you waiting on him to go first?" Brody asked.

"Because." Kianti traced a design on the tablecloth. "Men always start looking for the exit when the word 'love' comes out of a woman's mouth. We have no problem with letting you guys say it first—works better that way."

Winton was still laughing, but a bit more softly. "Honey, did it ever occur to you that the guy could be terrified that *you'll* be the one who'd be looking for the exit?"

Kianti had no response. Winton leaned across the table to shake hands with Khan once his point had been made.

The lights across the ballroom doused in two rapid flashes before remaining dim. A lone gleam of light was directed toward the podium on the stage. Kianti sat straighter in her chair when she saw Therin behind the mic. She punched Brody's thigh when she heard him chuckle over her reaction.

"Thanks everyone for accepting the invite." Therin greeted the expansive crowd once conversation had silenced. "It's been my honor for the past five years to host this event. As many of you are aware, my involvement with EYES is quite diversified but it's *this* event that holds a special place. It's a very multifaceted gathering—there are so many important reasons for our coming together this evening. *Money*." He extended a hand and joined in when the crowd exploded into laughter.

"But seriously, everyone, we're all aware that one of the main reasons EYES is able to do all the incredible things it does is because of its membership." Therin hesitated while the crowd murmured its agreement. "Members who give their money—yes, but also whose existence in this organization provides a far more valuable element: support. Our vast numbers and the diversity of that support tell all the naysayers that EYES and every organization like it has a place—a necessary place in our society and in the future of our kids."

Applause filled the soft-lit room.

"In speaking to that value of membership, I'd like

to introduce you all to our newest member, General Shepard Yale, retired U.S. Marine Corps."

Another wave of applause along with a few calls of "Semper Fi" increased the room volume to a roar. The general made his way to the stage, accepting the greetings with smiles and gracious waves. Once the applause reached the minute mark, he raised his hands for silence.

"Education has taken on a new meaning for me since I've become a grandfather," he said, nodding toward his family, who was seated at the tables along the balcony level. "After my conversations with our Mr. Rucker here—" he turned and shook hands again with Therin "—I was impressed by the devotion I found in someone so young. This gave me confidence that the EYES organization especially would stand the test of time once old goats like me are long gone."

There was a warm rumble of laughter and the general went on to discuss what he hoped to bring to the organization. Members of the audience, however, gradually lost interest in the general's comments. It appeared that a scuffle was breaking out at one of the center tables near the front.

The general even quieted as the situation grew more uncontrolled. Soon, everyone's attention was on the table where Marley Terrio struggled over being put in handcuffs.

"What is this?" Therin had left his place a few feet behind the general and stepped to the edge of the stage. He waved for security that was already making their way to the table.

"Call off your dogs, Rucker!" The man attempting

to cuff Marley Terrio raised a badge. His partners followed suit.

Therin raised a hand toward security before they pounced on the badge holders. "Explanations, gentlemen. Fast."

The man closest to Terrio nodded at his partners. One produced a document from his inside jacket pocket.

"We have a warrant for the arrest of Marley Terrio! The charge—child pornography!"

Silence emerged only to be peppered then by whispers. Marley Terrio appeared to wilt and was unable to answer his wife's panicky questions. The three officials led the man not too gently from the ballroom.

Kianti found Therin on his rooftop. She approached him slowly. After a second's hesitation, she rubbed her hand across his shoulder. Therin's reflexes were quick. He grabbed her hand, squeezed and held it close to his cheek.

"I've known Marley Terrio since…hell, ten years, easy—maybe longer…" Therin's sleek brows were drawn close as his frown set deeper. "I can't even begin to describe how committed he is to what we do."

Kianti kissed his shoulder and then pressed her head to his jacket sleeve.

"He's one of the oldest members…" He shook his head. "Works like a grunt to get things done. He's always the first to volunteer on committees. Every year he's tireless in putting together a charity ball for the kids.…" Therin regarded the statement with disdain and then cursed viciously.

"Honey, could this be a mistake?" Kianti leaned next to him against the ledge.

"You don't know how much I pray it is. I can't shake what I saw in his eyes, Key," he admitted.

"Could've been shock."

"Because of surprise or because he got caught?" Therin couldn't fight off his cynicism.

"So you do believe he did this?"

After a moment's consideration, Therin shook his head quickly. "I won't condemn him. At least not until I've got all the facts."

Kianti eased a wayward tendril of hair behind her ear. "What a shame it had to happen here tonight when such great things were in the works." She flashed Therin a curious look when he laughed suddenly. She couldn't read his expression but could tell that he wasn't in a mood to explain his reaction.

"So what happens next?" she asked while squeezing his biceps in a reassuring fashion.

Therin bowed his head. "Guess we'll talk to his attorney and go from there."

She smiled, taking time to relish the gorgeous set to his profile. "I'll leave you to your work then." She didn't notice his gaze when she kissed his temple and moved to leave. He caught her hand before she saw him move.

"What are you doing?"

"You're so busy." She drew the lapels of her swing coat together. "You're about to be even busier and I don't want to be in your way."

Therin's smile was a mixture of playfulness and danger. "You're crazy if you think you're leaving me here by myself."

"Baby." Her deep gaze softened over his mood. "You've got to focus on this mess. You don't need me hanging around, especially when I have no idea about... the politics of politics, and I don't want one."

"I don't want one, either." His smile deepened while his grip on her hand tightened. Soon, they were leaving the rooftop.

"You've lost your mind!" Vaughn shouted. "The press is in an uproar. If you leave now, they'll be in a frenzy, and I damn well don't want to be stuck in the middle of it!"

Therin brought a hand down to Vaughn's rigid shoulder. "Cut the act, V. You know you live for this shit, so don't try foolin' me. Besides, Gary, Peter and Morgan are here to shield you from some of it."

"Hell, Morgan's MIA. I haven't talked to him all day."

"I hadn't noticed...seemed excited about hearing Kianti play." Therin's voice held an absent quality as he was more focused on the outraged crowd. "Anyway, I'm about to get lost," he said, taking note of the reporters pointing toward him and Vaughn.

Vaughn closed his eyes, understanding Therin's vague phrasing perfectly. "Don't do this to me, man."

"That's why you get paid the big bucks." Therin clapped Vaughn's shoulder again and winked before making a hasty exit.

He found Kianti shortly after arriving in the packed foyer. Conversation and questions were thrown at him in a crazed manner, but Therin wasn't swayed by any of it. Focusing on Kianti, and the way she radiated calm amidst the tempest, allowed him to block the events of the past hour. He committed himself to enjoying a stolen moment with the woman he loved.

The lobby of the downtown hotel that housed Therin's penthouse apartment was pretty quiet for the hour. Of course, that had a lot to do with the fact that many who resided in the building were either guests at his event or tourists visiting Vancouver and probably out enjoying the night life of the city.

"Fritz." Therin's greeting to the clerk was soft when he and Kianti approached the gleaming gray marble front desk. He kept her close while signing in and collecting his mail.

Kianti couldn't help but wonder about his mood. He seemed cool enough, but she knew he had to be hurting. It had to be quite a blow to discover someone you admire may not be worthy of that admiration. She didn't believe he'd want to discuss it further that evening, so she remained silent and decided to take her cues from him.

Therin's "cues" weren't difficult to follow. He didn't bother with turning up the lights in the apartment. He tossed his keys to the message desk, pulled Kianti closer and treated her to a deep kiss.

She melted the second his tongue swirled about her own and teased it into an erotic play. She was happy to let him take the lead, which he did with great zeal. There in the foyer, he took her out of her dress while simultaneously doffing his own things. Their clothing was left in a pool on the floor when he carried her to his bedroom.

An added intensity flavored their time together that night. Kianti recognized it as frustration—no doubt over the fiasco that evening. Therin gave as much as he took and what he took was extensive. Low, hungry sounds vibrated from his throat and chest while his mouth traveled freely across her body. When she tried to touch him, he laced his fingers between hers and kept her a prisoner beneath him on the bed that was becoming increasingly tangled. There was a savage urgency in the way he feasted on her nipples. He left them rigid and glistening wet from his attention for only a brief time while he dropped wet kisses to the undersides of her breasts.

Kianti strained against his hold as his mouth worked relentlessly against her. She sobbed into the coverings when he turned her to her stomach and resumed his ravenous feasting upon her back and shoulders.

She thought she'd lose her mind when he nibbled at her hipbone while curving a hand around her waist and thrusting his fingers inside her quivering body. She eased her legs apart to offer him more room to play with her and her hips bucked softly against his mouth until he bit down gently to urge her still.

Kianti had no complaints about the way he handled her, especially when his nibbles at her hip traveled lower around the curve of her derriere and the valley between. She orgasmed as his thumb worked her clit in the midst of his tongue treating her bottom to the most intimate exploration.

Still, Therin would allow her no real control during the moment. When he applied protection and took her from behind, she silently prayed that he wouldn't tone down the heat of their encounter. Her sobs into the covers gained volume as another wave of satisfaction claimed her. She was seconds away from climax, when he turned the tables and tugged her over him.

Kianti bit her lip, feeling much like an inexperienced virgin then. It wasn't long though before the realization of control took hold and she helped herself. Her hair had tumbled from its elegantly confined upsweep long ago. Now, it hung down her back as she treated him and herself to the slow, heated up and down movements of her sex on his.

Her moans were repetitive and in perfect rhythm with the way she rode him. Therin's hold on her hips was loose; all his strength was in the part of his anatomy she'd taken command of. Giving into her determination to take him until he was depleted, Therin buried the heels of his hands against his eyes. He chanted her name and met her every stroke with a thrust. When he tried to reclaim dominance, she changed the rotation of his hips and contracted her inner walls around him. His groan held a tinge of surrender that brought a triumphant smile to her face. Convinced that he was at last driven down by the force of her desire, she clutched and released his length wickedly and relentlessly until they were coming sweetly, blissfully, simultaneously....

Chapter 15

Therin had been awake over an hour simply watching Kianti as she slept. He liked the look of it. What's more, he liked the look of her doing it in his bed. He knew he wanted to enjoy the image for more than just one night. He wanted more than just the series of stolen moments that made up the foundation of their brief acquaintance.

He leaned over to toy with the hair curled about her neck. He tugged several locks free and rubbed them between his thumb and forefinger to relish the heavy healthy feel of it against his skin.

She murmured his name during her slumber and he smiled as she snuggled deeper into the covers.

He loved her. He loved her and it had happened so peacefully, so subtly yet it hadn't gone unnoticed. He'd embraced every moment of it. He could actually feel himself falling willingly into the midst of it.

She snuggled a bit deeper into the covers and Therin

decided to give her peace. Gingerly, he left the bed, craving a hot cup of coffee. He walked barefoot through the apartment, which was illuminated by the predawn light streaming past the tall living room windows. He switched on the lamp in the center of a small round breakfast table and saw one of Kianti's CDs lying there. In the top corner of the case, there was a sticky note carrying the words *Play Me.*

Therin obliged, knowing a dose of her exquisite piano playing would only make the morning better. He eased the disc into the changer system tucked in the shelving near the table. Yawning then, he massaged sleep from his neck and shoulders while heading over to start the coffee.

Instead of Kianti's music lofting from the changer, a computer-generated voice emerged.

"She's very beautiful, Rucker. Looks like she's the one who truly belongs in your bed. It'd be a shame to let your stubbornness ruin her."

Therin stood still for what had to be a full minute. Stiffly, he managed to trudge over to the shelving. As though he expected it to burn to the touch, he tentatively reached out to hit the repeat button. A second after the message ended, he shut down the system.

Hand fisted to his mouth, he dropped into the nearest chair. His light eyes narrowed toward the changer. He ejected the CD, studied it solemnly and then broke it in half.

"Therin?"

An hour later, Kianti took the same route to the kitchen that her lover had when his mind was on a hot cup of coffee. She tapped her fingers to the counter and looked around.

"Therin?" she called again when the atmosphere of silence became too much for her liking. She was turning to leave the kitchen when she noticed the broken CD on the table. Before she could touch the shards, there was the distinct click of locks in the distance. Kianti rushed out, expecting to find Therin coming through the front door. Nothing prepared her to see Brody, Winton, Khan and Cube entering instead. Reflexively, she tightened her hold on the sheet that covered her.

"Get dressed." Brody was cool in the wake of the confusion he saw in her eyes. "We'll explain."

"Explain now." She came down off the last step leading to the living room from the kitchen.

"Honey, Brody's right, why don't you—" Khan raised his hands defensively at the look she slanted him.

"Explain," she said, having turned back to Brody.

"Rucker called us to come get you," he said.

"What happened?"

"He just told us to come for you." Brody shrugged. "He didn't seem upset."

"That damned party," she muttered, biting on her thumbnail then. "Everything's such a mess. He's got a lot on his plate." She fixed the guys with an apologetic look. "He didn't need to call you, I'm fine."

"Key—"

"Really, Winton, I'm fine and I don't need you guys hovering."

"Honey, come with us." Brody moved closer.

She laughed. "Honestly, Brody, I'll be just fine here with Therin."

"Dammit, Key!" Cube quieted himself and took a deep breath to calm down. "Baby, he doesn't want you here."

"What?" Her voice sounded strong enough. Still, something in the way Cube spoke the words sent a queasiness through her stomach.

The others sent glares in Cube's direction.

"Rucker told us he had too much going on to handle this," Brody said then.

"Handle…this?"

"Your sickness, honey," Khan clarified and then ran a hand across his close-cut blue-black hair. "He said he'd made a mistake thinking he could deal with it day in and day out."

"Son of a bitch," Cube growled.

"Cube, chill." Winton clapped his friend's shoulder. "Better for him to say it now than later after something happens.…"

"Screw that." Cube shook off Winton's hand. "Don't make him out to be all gracious and shit, Wint. The fool flat-out told us how much he was enjoyin' the sex, but it wasn't good enough to risk her dyin' on him."

Kianti felt her stomach curdle then. She felt the strength leaving her legs, but she refused to collapse in front of them.

"You okay?" Brody had taken note of her hand braced to the back of the sofa.

The guys silenced their ranting to observe her.

"Key?"

"Brody, please." She waved a hand. "I'll be ready to go in a second."

* * *

"Ms. Lawrence!"

Kianti and the guys were making their way out to the lobby for an early checkout when they were stopped by Bose Cooper, one of EYES's lead members.

"Bose Cooper, Ms. Lawrence. I must say that my wife and I are great fans. We especially enjoyed your performance last night." Bose squeezed one of her hands in both of his beefy ones.

She managed a smile that didn't manage to reach her eyes. "I appreciate that, Mr. Cooper. I'm sorry things turned out so terribly last night." She cleared her throat on the ball of emotion that had formed over the loaded statement.

Bose nodded, his expression had taken on a somber sheen as well. "Which brings me to my point of stopping you all like this." He made contact with the four men standing behind her. "We're hoping to salvage something good from last night's fiasco—a more intimate gathering."

Kianti nodded.

"We'd be honored if you'd join us."

The smile Kianti had worked to uphold, faltered then. "Mr. Cooper, we—"

"I understand this is all very sudden. We'd be honored if you'd at least consider giving us an extra night. We're hoping to put together something more intimate than last night's affair. A cocktail party slash concert exclusively for EYES members."

Brody moved in closer then. "Mr. Cooper, Ms. Lawrence's health tends to wear out on her—wear her down, if you understand my meaning. We'd like to get her home—"

"Brody." Kianti patted his chest and offered him a pitiful smirk before she turned back to Bose Cooper. "Would you excuse us for a minute, Mr. Cooper?"

"Please tell us you're not considering doing this?" Winton said once they had moved a ways down the hall for a bit more privacy.

"I can't let my personal issues get in the way of what's important." Her voice shook with uncertainty, though the look in her eyes was firm.

Cube muttered a curse. "What's important is your health." The scowl he wore made him look even more intimidating.

She lowered her head and sighed. "This is a worthy cause and if I can do something to help support it, then I feel obligated to try, at least."

Khan rolled his eyes and turned away. Winton and Cube followed suit.

Kianti sighed at their behavior and then turned to Brody. "I promise I'm all right to do this," she told him, taking a moment to massage her neck when her doctor walked off to join is coworkers.

"Mr. Cooper?" She headed back toward the man waiting at the other end of the corridor. "I'd love to be a part of the event."

"Wonderful!" The man clapped his hands together once. "We're very grateful. There will be a lunch meeting at 3:00 p.m. with the other musicians—some who are just fresh in town from other jobs—*gigs.*" He smiled bashfully. "We figured it'd be fruitful to give you all some time together beforehand to discuss pieces and possible collaborations."

"Sounds good."

"The meeting will be at the hotel restaurant, The Vista—sixth floor."

Kianti nodded and shook hands once again with Bose before he headed off.

"We don't believe you're willin' to stick around here another damn night for this," Khan grumbled once he and the others had crowded around again.

Kianti smoothed a curl behind her ear. "Well, I am so…could I please have someone's room key? Think I'll take a nap before this meeting."

"Take mine." Brody dug out the card from the back pocket of his trousers. Room 8710. I'll be up to check on you soon."

Alone in the elevator, Kianti toyed with pushing for the floor to Therin's room. She shook off the notion and cursed herself for having it. That ship had sailed. Unfortunately, it had taken her heart along with it.

Later that day, Kianti was happy she had decided to participate in the concert, if only for the chance to take part in the lunch meeting with the other musicians. The gathering was crowded and lighthearted. Many were excited by the idea of the concert and cheered the organization for not letting the drama from the previous evening sway them from their cause. Several people had already sectioned themselves off, having chosen to do special performances together.

"How did you hear about this?" Kianti was asking Shelton Innes, who had already claimed her as his pianist.

Shelton nodded toward the server who had just returned with extra dressing for his salad. "We had a gig in Chi-Town. The EYES drama was all over the news." He shrugged while drowning lettuce, tomatoes and cucumber in a mound of Ranch dressing. "Geary's aunt's a member," he said, referring to his group's bass player. "She told him about what they were trying to do and asked if we might be willing to make a stop through."

"It's been a real mess," Kianti noted, blowing a tuft of hair from her eyes and she looked around the room. "The event had all the makings of a real success before all that happened. So where's everyone else?"

"Trying to snag a vocalist. We don't just want a host of instrumental pieces. Give 'em a little variety."

Kianti's expression was melancholy. "Thanks, Shelton, for asking me to sit in. I wasn't up for doing a solo."

"Whatever." Shelton rolled his eyes and chomped down a mouthful of the drenched salad. "You knew we wouldn't, *couldn't* leave you out there like that." His brows rose as he sighed. "I was a little surprised though."

Kianti halted her juice bottle halfway to her mouth. "Surprised?"

"To find you lookin' so down. Thought you'd be on cloud nine right about now."

"Why?"

"Well, this is your boy's event, right? The ambassador." Shelton's lashes fluttered in a playful manner.

Kianti couldn't help but laugh. "Well…the drama at the event wasn't the only drama of the weekend."

Shelton raised a hand. "Say no more. Just be ready to play your butt off tonight—drive out all that drama."

Kianti tilted her bottle in mock toast. She was hoping to do just that.

Bose Cooper was obviously a man proud of his accomplishment. Understandably, he was eager to boast of the surprise concert to his colleagues. He'd arranged for his EYES associates to drop in on the lunch meeting as the gathering reached its end. Sadly, not every one of Bose's associates shared his excitement over the event.

"What the hell?" Therin's bright stare was noticeably harsh when it settled on Kianti across the room with Shelton Innes.

"...we even have several performers who we were unable to pull in for last night's program," Bose was saying as he answered excited inquiries from the group who joined him at The Vista. "We've got quite a variety of musical styles and—"

"Excuse us, folks." Therin clutched Bose's arm and gave the man a firm tug.

"Therin—" Bose could say little else stunned as he was by Therin's behavior just then.

"What the hell is she doing here?"

Bose tilted his head. "I'm sorry, Therin, I don't—"

"Kianti Lawrence."

"Ah, Ms. Lawrence! Yes, I was especially proud of persuading her to join us."

"Bose, she was supposed to leave this morning." Therin groaned the words, massing the sudden ache at the bridge of his nose.

"I know!" Bose laughed, clapping Therin's back. "A damn lucky break, I'd say. A diverse as well as entertaining lineup, don't you think?"

"Right," Therin said, dejected.

Bose, at last, took note of his colleague's demeanor. "Therin? What is it, son? This is good news, you know?"

With everything going on, the last thing Therin wanted was to cause any further upset. He forced a grin to his face and laid a hand across Bose's. "You're right. It is. You should be proud of putting this thing together."

"Marley wouldn't want you worrying this way, son." Bose saw through the act Therin tried to put in place. "Think about tonight and have a good time, hmm?"

Therin allowed a curse to slip past his lips once Bose had moved on. Thinking about that night was all he'd be able to do. Unfortunately, thinking about that night in conjunction with having a party would be damn near impossible.

Kianti should have been headed far away from him by then. She should have been far away from him and hating him with a passion for what he'd done. He should have known this wouldn't be an easy thing.

He maintained a somewhat secluded spot near the dining room entrance and focused in on her. She appeared happy, laughing with her drummer friend, Shelton Innes. Therin grimaced, figuring the guy was about to be even more satisfied than he probably was at that very moment. Kianti was going to need a shoulder to cry on once he attacked her sensitive heart…again.

"Key…" Shelton called, directing his gaze above her head.

Kianti's laughter softened and she studied Shelton's

pointed expression for a moment before turning to see what had him so subdued.

The scent of Therin's cologne had her swallowing around an emotional ball that had formed in her throat even before she looked up into his face. She could only hold eye contact for a split second before she looked away.

Shelton cleared his throat and quietly made his exit. Kianti didn't notice he'd gone. She didn't notice much of anything except that Therin was within touching distance. After all that had happened, she couldn't make herself forget the feel of his body against hers.

"May I talk to you?"

"You can do whatever you like and you seem to take a lot of enjoyment in it," she muttered, turning her back on him in the chair she occupied.

"I expected you to be gone already." Therin kept his voice as cold and as guarded as his gaze.

Kianti folded her arms over her chest. "Sorry to disappoint you. Don't worry, though. The guys gave me your message. I got it loud and clear."

He took the seat Shelton had left vacant. "Then you understand?"

She could have laughed over his nerve. "Don't worry yourself, Therin, I'm not hanging around to appeal to your sensitivity. You've shown me what you're made of."

Her words cut Therin deeper than they would have had he actually deserved them. Somehow he managed to hold on to his aloofness.

"I could say the same." He slid a pointed glance toward Shelton, who was across the dining room talking with his group and a few other musicians. "You seem to be moving on."

"You're an ass." She barely raised a brow. "If you don't mind leaving now? I think I've let you waste enough of my time." She feigned sudden interest in the contents of her coffee mug and tried to wait him out.

When Therin left the table, she forbid herself to cry.

The impromptu concert party was a success. There was varied conversation among the crowd regarding the scandal rocking the organization and the arrest of Marley Terrio. Thankfully, the unrest was tempered by a slew of great performances.

Most of the performances were artist's collaborations. Only a few acts performed new work. Kianti had hoped her appearance with Shelton and the group from Scottie's would suffice. The audience wanted more. Not to be outdone by the other acts who'd shared original efforts, Kianti gave the audience a taste of her own original piece, "Stolen Moment."

Of course, Therin was a part of the audience. After their *chat* earlier that day, he'd decided to remain absent from the evening's festivities. The decision held up all of five minutes. Taking in the beautifully haunting melody she'd first played for them during their private moment together, it was all he could do to remain there and toss back one gin and tonic after another.

Kianti took her bows and Therin headed out. Something led him backstage. To do what, he had no clue. When he got there, however, her back was toward him and she was crying.

Instinctively, Therin made a move toward her but he stopped himself short.

By the time Kianti had sensed she wasn't alone and turned, he was gone.

"Where is she?"

Brody grimaced and looked over at Kianti slumped on the passenger side of his Denali. "She's sleeping."

"Where is she?"

"Hell, man, isn't it better to just break it off clean?"

Therin muttered something foul.

"We're driving her back to her place in Dakota." Brody's tone was clipped.

"How is she?"

"I gave her something to help her sleep."

"Good." Therin sighed on the other end of the phone line. "Good... Does she hate me?"

Brody's resulting laughter was short and without a trace of humor. "We said everything we could think of to make sure she does. Are you sure that's the way you want it?" he asked after silence met his words.

"No." There was another indecipherable mutter of a curse. "But the last thing I want is to have her hurt over this."

"And isn't that just what you're managing with this stunt of yours?

"Listen, Brody, thanks," Therin said once he'd considered Brody's words for half a minute. "Thank the fellas for helping me take care of it this way." He ended the connection without another word.

"They've got him on suicide watch," Marley Terrio's attorney, Claude Pressman, explained as he and Therin followed the guard to a conference room where they were to meet with the man.

"Suicide watch." Therin clutched Claude's arm. A frown darkened his features when the older man smiled and shook his head.

"Just for show, kid."

"Did he do this, Claude?"

Claude's expression darkened.

"Then what the hell is he doing in here?" Therin hissed.

Claude nodded toward the guard who was heading farther down the iron-bar-lined corridor. "We decided it was best to take advantage of this opportunity," he whispered once he and Therin had fallen back in step behind the guard. "Out of sight, out of the prying eyes of the press and others…give us time to work on our strategy." His expression harbored a smug undercurrent. "Right now the opposition's waiting on our move. Let 'em wait."

Therin massaged new tension from his neck and loosened the black tie he wore. He followed Claude into a fluorescent-lit concrete room. The tension he'd attempted to ease from his neck renewed itself when he saw Marley Terrio waiting in shackles and a gray jumpsuit.

"It's all right, son." Marley's shackles clattered when he raised a hand to quiet Therin's outraged curses.

"What the devil is this shit all about?" Therin tamped down his anger until the guard walked out. His temper was already in a frightful state and answers were of the utmost importance.

"Is Claude right? Are you planning to wait? To hide

out here and do nothing except give people the impression these accusations are true?"

Marley and Claude exchanged shrugs.

"Until we can figure out a better way," Marley said. "Don't worry, son. We've got a lot of heads working on this. We've been in this game a long time, kid. If sacrificing ourselves turns out to be best for the greater good of the organization, then so be it. We'll take our chances."

Therin studied the men in disbelief and then slumped back in the steel chair he occupied. " I just don't get why this is such a hot button for these fools. I mean, did they all hate school as kids?" He left the chair as quickly as he'd claimed it.

Marley chuckled as Therin paced. "Ah, Claude... remember how it felt to be that young and idealistic?"

Claude let out a satisfied grunt. "Good times, good times..."

Therin turned with disbelief filling his eyes. "I'm glad to find you so jovial behind bars."

Marley sobered and smoothed one hand over the other. "Therin, it all goes back to what you just said. Education *is* a hot button. I've seen evidence of that before *and* during my time working for EYES."

"But for these idiots to go to such lengths to shut us down?"

"Therin, son, you've seen it yourself. Education is always the first pot to dip out of when the budget's in trouble. Everything else is more important than it is. But what if that belief started to shift?" Marley wagged a finger in Therin's direction.

"What if the thought of a child's education stirred

the hearts of those who never before took stock of its true worth?" Marley looked over at Claude who nodded his agreement. "What if that *thought* filled them with passion? A passion for education. The educating of a child's mind—the nurturing which could inevitably affect change on the grandest scales."

"That's terrifying to some folks, Therin," Claude interjected. "To have the masses see the true importance of education over corporate aspirations, military endeavors…scary stuff…"

"And to have young champions such as yourself leading the crusade, is the cherry on top." Marley slapped his hand against the cold chrome table he sat behind. "You've already got the support from stuffy old coots like Claude and me. But then there's the glamour set from the movie and music communities—talk about affecting change on a grand scale!" Marley reclined in the uncomfortable chair and held the look of a man at ease. "Sure, I was terrified when those fools slapped cuffs on me over that concocted nonsense. But I'd gladly take the heat if it means keeping you guys in play."

"What will you do?" Therin asked once he'd considered the man's opinion.

Marley grinned. "What I've always done, son. Ride out the storms. One comes round every five to ten years or so. 'Course I'm getting older now so I tend to expect them every two to three years."

The words sparked Claude's infectious laughter. Therin wasn't immune, yet the humor didn't quite reach his eyes when he laughed.

Chapter 16

From his office window, Therin stared down at the Vancouver traffic. He couldn't see anything but Kianti's face. His focus was on her, as it had been for the two weeks since he'd brought an end to their involvement. She hadn't tried to contact him, but then he hadn't expected that she would. She was too gracious…and tough for that.

She had accepted his wishes without argument and any second thoughts on his part were moot then. He was certain her hatred for him ran deep. That was the way he wanted it…right?

Rick Dubose had stopped talking about the speech he was drafting. It didn't take much for him to tune in to the fact that his boss was in another world.

Rick closed the folder he'd brought to the meeting. The crinkling of the papers must have brought Therin's attention back to the matter at hand. He turned and fixed his speechwriter with a sheepish look.

"Sorry, man, you think we could do this later?"

"No problem." Rick was already standing to collect the rest of his things, which were spread out across the coffee table he was using. "Can I make a suggestion, though?"

Therin waved a hand and turned back to glare out the windows.

"Take a break," Rick urged, stacking his folder and pens to the laptop he'd brought along.

Therin bowed his head as a smirk curved his mouth. "Thought I'd been doin' all right pretending I'm good."

"Sorry, sir, but you're no good at pretending." Rick's tone was playful.

"I should've asked you before I tried it." Therin laughed. He folded his arms over the gray pinstriped shirt he wore and leaned against the sill.

"That's what friends and speechwriters are for." Rick gathered up his things. "You just need to get lost."

"What?" Therin's sleek brows drew a smidge closer.

"Get lost," Rick called over his shoulder as he made his way to the office door. "Go someplace and clear your head, hide out for a few days—heck, a few weeks. Get away from the press and all this drama."

"Sounds like good advice."

"Hmph." Rick turned the doorknob. "I suggest you jump on it because good advice doesn't come out of my mouth very often."

Rick was gone soon after. Alone then, Therin collapsed to the edge of his desk.

"Jesus," he whispered.

* * *

Brody walked into the kitchen in time to see Kianti taking her pill. His surprise was unmistakable and Kianti dissolved into laughter at the sight of it.

"Did I just miss out on a chance to see one of the guys bullying you?" he asked, coming to lean against the counter.

"No." She set aside the water glass while shaking her head. "I've just been taking all this time to put things in some kind of perspective."

Brody hid his hands in his jean pockets and stepped closer. "Rucker have anything to do with it?"

"At first," she admitted and took a seat at the break-fast nook. "But even then I was still against taking the pills."

"So what changed?"

"Me." She propped both fists beneath her chin and smiled serenely. "I always let that feeling of being dif-ferent…of being *less* overshadow what was really im-portant—my health, my life. Once I stopped to think about that, I realized what I was a slave to hadn't been the pills, but letting myself feel belittled by having to take them."

Brody's mouth twisted into a smirk that gave him the look of being impressed. "Who are you and what have you done with Kianti Lawrence?" He sobered quickly once they'd shared a laugh. He moved over to pull Kianti into a hug. "I'm proud of you." He kissed the top of her head.

Kianti relished the hug. She'd shied away from close-ness over the past two weeks. She knew the guys had noticed the change in her demeanor. It wasn't hard to do as she was usually the one initiating so many of the hugs and kisses that flowed between them on a daily basis.

The closeness made her think of Therin. She'd made a promise to herself to forget him, which was useless as well as stupid. Why would she want to forget one of the sweetest times in her life? She squeezed her eyes shut and snuggled deeper into Brody's embrace. It was better all around to shut out such memories. However, it was well-known that doing what was best wasn't her strong suit.

Gary and Peter sent Therin a knowing look across the table where the staff meeting had just taken place. Ruby Loro was last to leave and had just shut the conference room door behind herself.

"V, man? Do you have a few minutes?" Therin asked just as Vaughn was rolling his chair back from the table.

"What's up?" Vaughn obliged, slanting quick glances toward Peter and Gary.

"Why'd you do it, V?"

"Come again?" Vaughn fixed his oldest friend with a confused look.

Therin's smile was small while he studied his friend. "No one but you knows what I mean when I say I'm 'getting lost.'" He looked up in time to see clarity emerge in Vaughn's eyes.

"Those were the very words I used the night I left the party with Kianti. You knew I meant I was heading to the apartment."

"You're paranoid, you know that, right?" Vaughn

chuckled, though his nervousness was evident. "All this mess going on's got you paranoid as hell."

"Let's talk about 'all this mess.'" Therin maintained his reclining position in the chair at the end of the table. "Ruby didn't tell a soul what she'd done when she first got to the country. But checking backgrounds is your job and you're too good to let somethin' like that slip past you. You knew, didn't you?"

Vaughn refused to answer one way or another.

"Then there's the comment made by Rick's attacker."

"Now hold up a damn minute! You don't think I—"

"The way it was said. Rick thought a staff member may've attacked him."

"This is craziness!" Vaughn stood. "I can't believe you're losin' it with me—me of all people!"

"Don't play me for a fool any more than you already have. I'm way too pissed off to deal with it."

"Drop it, T. You're only pissed off over Kianti leaving. Hell, get over it—there'll be others."

"Every bit of it points to you."

"What?" Vaughn slammed his palms down on the table. "Some coincidences involving the staff, a CD and you making some cryptic comment about the condo?"

Therin smoothed both hands over his head. "I didn't mention a CD. How do you know about that, V?"

The silence then was heavy, yet meaningful. Therin waited to see whether his oldest friend would take responsibility or play the innocent. Apparently, Vaughn Burgess decided on a combination of both.

"Is it so difficult for you to give an inch, here? To share the wealth?"

"And who shares the wealth with us?" Therin's brittle temper snapped.

"To hell with you, Therin! Idealistic and proud—closed off to what all of your good intentions do to those on the sidelines of your life."

"The staff knew what they were in for when they came to work for me." Therin left his chair.

Again, Vaughn slammed his hands down to the table. "Dammit, Ther, not your staff! Your friends. Hell, your own damn family!"

Therin's shoulders stiffened and he turned.

Gary and Peter exchanged looks across the table.

"What, Vaughn? What about my family?" Therin's voice had softened to a deadly whisper. "What do you know about my parents?"

Vaughn's anger wilted into a bit of disbelief. "Are you asking— Are you accusing me of having something to do with—"

"Did you?"

"Son of a bitch!" Vaughn kicked away his chair. "I don't have to put up with this shit!" He moved for the door only to have Gary and Peter block his way. He looked toward Therin again.

"You placin' me under arrest, Mr. Ambassador?"

"They're taking you to your office." Therin nodded toward Peter and Gary. "Clean it out. You're fired."

"Hmph." Vaughn's lip curled into a snarl and he regarded Therin with nasty intent. "All we tried to do to get you to break, to play ball, and the only thing it took was us threatening your latest piece of ass."

"Come on, Vaughn." Gary tugged the sleeve of his suit jacket.

Vaughn jerked away. "And she's a prime piece, don't get me wrong, Ther."

"Get him out of here," Therin growled.

"Does she play a tune for you once you've screwed her brains out?"

Therin leapt across the table. He snagged the front of Vaughn's shirt in one hand and used the other to slam his fist into his jaw. Gary and Peter's combined efforts broke Therin's vise grip minutes later.

Despite a busted lip, Vaughn struggled to break away from Gary and Peter as they pulled him out of the conference room.

"You're just a small fish, Therin! These folks play to win! They won't stop until EYES is done, finished, over! I'm the least of your problems!"

"Get him out!" Therin's fist hit the table, threatening to splinter it.

Outside her home, Kianti shook the snow from her black ski boots. She'd been standing in the same spot for almost seven minutes and had only just realized that her feet were numb despite the fur insulation.

Of course, thoughts of Therin were to blame. It had become increasingly difficult to keep her mind off him since the guys had returned to California. She knew it was unhealthy and that she had to get over it—over him. A few more days of moping and then it was back to the land of the living, she swore to herself.

A crunch in the otherwise-silent early evening caught her ear. She whirled around to find Therin making his way toward her.

"They threatened me with you," he said when there

were only a few feet separating them. "They threatened me with you, Key." His voice was hushed that time as he lifted his hands in a show of defenselessness.

"Hmph." She rolled her eyes and studied him with disdain. "You should've asked the guys not to be so honest when they told me what you said. I already know the truth."

Therin smiled. "The truth, right…" He took a small step closer. "About how I thought I could handle it, but I couldn't. How the sex was incredible but I couldn't take knowing you could die on me."

She gasped.

"I knew I couldn't get you to leave me any other way. If I'd told you someone had gotten into the condo while we slept that morning and left a threat on your life, I'd have never gotten you to go, would I?"

"So instead you…*arranged* for my friends—my… my family to hurt me that way?"

"It was stupid, but I was afraid. It's true," he confirmed when she watched him in disbelief. Again, he stepped closer. "Knowing you're alive and hating me is way more acceptable than having you dead. You may not approve of my methods, Kia. Hell…*I* don't approve of them, but they were all I had."

Kianti pressed a hand to her throat to hold back a sob. "Couldn't you have trusted me to—to let you handle—"

"No. No, baby, I couldn't."

But for the limbs snapping and the brush creaking beneath the weight of the snow, there was silence.

"My parents died in a car accident. I never thought it was an accident." He walked past her to look out over the property. "It happened about two years after I got the ambassador's post. Just after I connected with EYES."

Kianti hugged herself and observed the rigid set of his broad shoulders as he talked.

"I brought a lot of big names on board with me when I came to the organization. It was the first real exposure the group got on a...cultural stage." He shrugged. "They'd been around for years, but in the shadows." He kicked at a stone with the tip of a black hiking boot.

"When I brought in my *friends,* it was suddenly cool to support education. The notice brought in tons of money. A lot of people didn't like that. I had no idea how much, not even when the threats started. Then my parents..." He began to rub his hand rapidly back and forth across his forehead as though that would drive out the memories. He turned back to Kianti.

"I didn't take threats seriously back then. I'll never make that mistake again. Never again with someone I love."

She blinked. "Someone you...what?"

"I love you." He laughed but the gesture carried no amusement. "I love you, Kianti, and I should have told you that a very long time ago. Instead, I played this stupid game and wound up having you hate me."

He stood there looking so rattled and Kianti could only stand there hugging herself as she absorbed all that he'd said. Her heart pounded and not from anything having to do with illness—far from it. She was opening her mouth to confess the emotions she'd held back long enough.

Therin grunted suddenly. Before Kianti could say a word, he crumpled to the ground right before her eyes.

Chapter 17

The snow was thick and freezing, but his chest felt on fire. The fiery feeling however soon vanished, right along with the biting cold as the feeling left his arms and legs. Barely, he managed to turn his head and saw the red ooze staining the white. He'd been shot.

Kianti's face eased into his line of vision and he smiled. She looked terrified. Therin thought she was the loveliest thing he'd ever seen. He closed his eyes.

"Therin? Therin!" She was calling him, frantically shoving at his chest until she snatched her hands away not wanting to injure him further. "Therin, baby, please…" she whispered lightly, slapping his cheeks. She pulled off the fuzzy brown mittens and pressed her fingertips to either side of his neck to feel for a pulse.

"Please, God…please." Her tone was soft, panicky. Quickly she glanced around for any sign of the shooter. Her first thought was that someone was out hunting and Therin got caught in the line of fire. She knew that wasn't it.

"Therin? Therin, honey, come on. Wake up now. Wake up." She added a bit more force behind the slaps to his cheeks. They had to get going. Who knew how close the shooter was. Shooters? She wouldn't think of that.

"Kia…"

Therin was moaning and frowning intermittently. Gradually, he came round, responding to her calls and slaps to his face.

"Baby, I have to get you out of here." *I have to get us out of here.*

Kianti sat back on her legs and studied him writhing in the snow. She fought to keep her confidence high while trying to calculate his weight. He was at least six feet tall and built like a wall of lean muscle.

Good luck lifting this specimen, girl.

"Therin?" she called again, applying the slaps to his cheek. "Therin, honey?" She smiled when his brilliant hazel gaze was focused on her face.

Awareness flooded his eyes as it seemed to register within him that their situation was dire.

"Honey, we've got to move." Kianti pushed her hair beneath the black and brown toboggan she wore. Rising to her feet, she gripped his hands and tugged. "Therin, we've got to go." She wouldn't look at the blood and commanded the firmness to remain in her voice.

She attempted to pull him up, but only managed to land on her rump in the snow. Crawling around behind him, she hooked her hands beneath his arms and linked them together in front of his chest.

"Honey, please." She encouraged a small measure of assistance, pressing a kiss to his temple. "That's it, that's it, baby." She celebrated his weak attempt to brace against her and rise.

She kept looking around for the shooter, but there was no movement or sound of snow crunching underfoot save theirs.

Therin was on his feet eventually. The bulk of his weight, however, rested on Kianti, and she had to plant her feet firmly before taking each step.

"You could…move more quick—quickly without me." He winced, recognizing the futility of their current rate of speed. "You could bring help."

"To do what?" She tightened her hold on his jacket. "To see to a dead man? That's a stupid idea, so unless you've got better words of encouragement, shut up and lean on me."

Wren set aside the basket of freshly folded towels she'd just brought up from the laundry room. She smoothed her hands across the sleeves of her blue-and-green flannel shirt while moving closer to the windows over the kitchen sink.

She frowned. It was impossible to miss the red streams staining the snow in a lengthy trail. Seconds after the discovery, she heard heavy banging on the back door.

"Vern!" Cautiously, Wren peeked out the curtain covering the window cut into the back door. "Vern!" she cried again while opening the door to Therin and Kianti.

"Jesus," Vern called when he ran into the kitchen. He arrived just in the nick of time.

Whatever strength had been driving Kianti gave out just then. Therin fell right into Vernon's arms and Kianti fell right against Wren.

"What happened?"

"I don't know! I just looked outside, saw the blood... Lord..."

"Calm yourself, love." Vern maintained the cooler head while hefting Therin against him. "Get her to that chair," he instructed his wife while he settled Therin to the sofa on the other side of the kitchen.

"I'm fine, Wren." Kianti felt her well-being improve the instant she sat down. Still, Wren worked feverishly, assuring herself that Kianti hadn't been wounded. "Therin's been shot, help Vern." Kianti squeezed the woman's hand. "Please, Wren."

Wren gave a quick nod and then ran over to see to the men. Kianti made her way slowly toward the sofa. She stopped halfway, too terrified to go forward and too terrified to turn back.

"I need my bag," Vern said, grimacing at the clothing that was matted to Therin's skin by the now-congealing blood. "Wren..."

While Vernon spoke to his wife about the things he'd need to assist Therin, Kianti drew on her courage and went to the sofa. Gently, she brushed her hand along Therin's face, sobbing then as she leaned close to kiss his cheek and jaw.

"Hang on, please hang on for me..."

"Count on it," Therin grunted even as a faint smile

curved his mouth. "No way am I dying and missing out on all this…pampering."

Kianti gushed, unashamed, crying and laughing at once.

"Shh…it's all right, it's all right," Therin soothed, though he seemed contented by her emotional display. "Mmm…you're gonna have to cool it, you know? Vern can only see to one of us at a time and I've got first dibs."

"Therin? I've got something here that'll make you woozy—very woozy," Wren said as she and Vern returned to work on the wound. Silence settled as she administered the shot.

"Good news," Vern called once he'd cut away Therin's jacket and shirts. "Looks like the bullet went straight through." He examined more closely while nodding. "Yep, straight through, and I can't see where anything vital's been hit."

Tensions eased at the news. Vernon and Wren worked diligently over the patient. They found the bullet that went through Therin's side, lodged in the heavy padding of the jacket he'd been wearing.

Kianti tried to remain standing close by to offer whatever assistance Vernon and Wren might need. It was clear that she was worn down and completely out. She didn't argue when Wren bullied her into one of the cushiony recliners in the den off from the kitchen.

"You're quite a woman, you know?" Wren raved, tucking a heavy patchwork quilt around Kianti once she'd removed her boots so her feet could warm near

the fire. "You've just saved the life of the man you love."
She kissed Kianti's temple and left her.

The words filled Kianti with pride and, more important, strength. She smiled serenely and eased into a deep sleep in seconds.

Hours later, Therin woke and found himself looking up into Kianti's face. Smiling, he snuggled his head deeper into her lap. "Am I dead?" he asked.

"You're not," she confirmed.

"Hmph, and here I thought you were an angel."

"I am." She shrugged and caressed his mouth with her thumb. "But earthbound just now."

"I love—"

"I love you," she said first.

He chuckled weakly. "'Cause I took a bullet?"

Kianti rolled her eyes. "Well…it was a sexy gesture but I felt it was a tad much."

"I'm sorry." He'd scarcely completed the apology before her mouth was covering his.

A knock to the bedroom door interrupted them. It was Vernon and Wren come to check on their patient.

Therin reached out to take Vern's hand. "Thanks, man." He tugged on Wren's hand to bring her close and kiss her cheek.

"We've got company," Wren announced after tucking the covers in around Therin and Kianti.

Therin frowned when he saw the familiar face peek inside the opening of the door. "Morgan?" he called, attempting to push himself up before Kianti settled him back against her chest.

"Boss," Morgan Felts greeted. "Are you two all

right?" he asked Kianti, leaning over to squeeze her hand. "Sorry for not getting here earlier." He smirked at the confusion on their faces. "Guess I've been late all the way around. You even managed to take Vaughn down before I could get to him."

"Vaughn?"

"He was behind it," Therin answered Kianti, but his eyes never left Morgan's face. "The threat on you—everything. How did you know?" he asked Morgan.

"I started digging around after what happened with Ruby." Morgan took a seat in the armchair facing the bed. "I couldn't get that stage name of hers out of my head. Finally, I remembered where I heard it or, in this case, saw it. I got together with Vaughn one night for drinks at his place. I remember swiping a few of his... DVDs." He gave a meaningful nod toward Therin, not wanting to come right out and say "porn flicks" in front of Kianti.

Therin smirked. "Only a few?"

Morgan grinned in spite of himself. "All right already, so it was five. I only got around to watching two of them, though...one of the ones I grabbed was *Spanish Heat.*" He bit his lip on a curse. "Maybe if I'd gotten around to watching that one, we could have avoided all this crap. Vaughn had to know who she was when you hired her. He had those movies months before she even started."

Therin cursed, his eyes narrowing sharply when he moved and dull pain stabbed his side. "What brought you out here, Morg?"

"The two dudes who arrested Marley Terrio at the party? I was there, by the way. Excellent playing," he told Kianti, who beamed at the compliment. "Once Terrio was in police custody, they dipped and I followed them while they followed you." He looked around at the cozy paneled bedroom. "'Course I didn't know where *here* was until…"

"Thanks, man." Therin extended his hand to Morgan who held on to it for a time. "But we both know Vaughn and those fellas who arrested Terrio are small potatoes. There are *way* bigger fish behind this."

"Well, your boy Vaughn apparently knows that. I talked to Gary and Peter while we were waiting on you to wake up."

"What happened?" Therin watched as Morgan settled back in the chair.

"He tried playing the big dog 'til he saw U.S. Feds along with Vancouver's Finest. I never knew the man had such a lovely singing voice. Seems our high-powered elusive enemies were really a rather small faction of troublemakers with allegiance to politics as usual and obscene amounts of money being funneled into what benefits them most." He shrugged. "Sad to say education wasn't on their list." Morgan laced his fingers and studied them for a time. "Seems everybody on the *other side* isn't as loyal to education taking a backseat, as it would seem. More folks are realizing the importance of contributing to instead of castrating education budgets." He smirked on the words. "Rest of Vaughn's friends are either running for cover or trying to make deals. Some already spilled the beans about Marley Terrio being set up."

Therin winced while trying to move from where he

rested against Kianti. "But they're out of jail, right?" He referred to the senior EYES member.

"Released on bail a few days ago," Morgan confirmed. "Media's already been alerted. I'd say we're in for one helluva press conference in a few weeks."

"You think it'll all pan out?"

"I'm not naive but in this case I'd say more than a little luck's comin' our way. The two fools who came after you are dead—there won't be any questions," Morgan said to Kianti when she gasped. "The group I brought along with me helped to clean up the mess. New snow fallin' helped out, too. As for all the rest, folks are definitely listening—maybe what Vaughn spilled will lead us to the real idiots behind this."

"You two were such good friends. Why would Vaughn do something like this?" Kianti asked Therin.

"Money," Morgan said.

Therin shook his head. "Power. Vaughn always liked handling the press. Being the front man when I didn't feel up to the aggravation, which was usually most of the time. Guess he wanted a bigger piece of the pie— or the chance to make his *own* pie."

Kianti smoothed her hair behind her ear and frowned. "But to ruin your friendship…"

Therin mimicked her frown. "In politics, people do a lot worse for a whole lot less."

Vernon peeked into the room then. "Sorry, Mr. Felts—patient needs his rest."

"Right, doc." Morgan sent Vern a mock salute and pushed out of the armchair. "I'm here for the duration. We've got men posted all around the Shays and some back at Kianti's." He slapped hands with Therin and then took one of Kianti's hands in both of his.

"I didn't have the chance to fully enjoy that piano performance of yours. I'd love to request another."

She placed her hand on top of his. "Anytime, Morgan. Anytime."

"Thank you for saving my life, Ms. Lawrence," Therin was saying once the doors closed behind Morgan. "Slap some sense into me the next time I try to question your strength, all right?"

She laughed. "Remember you said that."

"I love you." He spoke in the midst of the tender kiss they shared.

She smoothed her hand along his sideburns. "You know I love you—very much."

"That's good." He tugged at a lock of her hair. "I really can't have you hating me if we're going to be married." He grinned, kissing her suddenly to take advantage of her lips, which were parted in surprise.

Chapter 18

Pacifica, California~One Week Later

"It's only a flesh wound."

"It was way more than that."

"It's not that now," Therin argued and leaned close to ply her with another kiss.

"Mmm...no." She resisted when he snuggled against her. "You can't overdo anything just yet."

He dropped his head to her shoulder and groaned. "You really expect us to share a bed and...sleep?"

"Not at all," she purred.

Seconds later, Therin found himself on his back. Kianti kissed her way down his neck, chest and torso, paying special attention to the ragged scar he now wore along the edge of his toned abdomen. She pleasured him shamelessly. Therin reveled in the feel of it and the sight of his ring glittering on her finger.

"Kia…" he groaned when she stopped much too soon. His disappointment vanished when she eased protection in place and took him inside her.

"Ah, ah, ah." She pressed her finger to his mouth. "Don't fight me. Remember, I've got permission to hit you if you dare question my strength."

Therin's chuckle ended on a groan. The moment passed in an erotic blur.

"So what'd the guys have to say about the engagement?" Therin asked later as they cuddled among the tangle of bed covers.

Kianti giggled on the memory of it. "They started arguing over which of them would give me away. I had to remind them that my dad had first dibs on that job. They'll be all right." She smiled while measuring the size of her hand against Therin's. "Now that I'm back on the pills, everyone's happy."

"Including you?" he asked, feeling her bristle a bit as she lay next to him.

"Yes. *Yes,*" she repeated, following a sigh. "It was like I told Brody, it wasn't the pills but giving in to the thought that I was weak for taking them."

"And here I thought it all had to do with me." Therin buried his handsome face in the crook of her neck.

"Well, it did." She turned over to face him. "Some of it did but in the end it was something I had to work through…for me." She traced her thumbnail across his collarbone. "I've only got one life, couldn't take a chance on missing the best part of it." She leaned close to treat him to a sweet kiss. She noticed the faraway look in his light eyes when she pulled back.

"You're thinking of your parents," she guessed.

He blinked, his expression mildly stunned. "How...?"

"You looked the same way when we were in North Dakota and you told me about what happened to them." She winced. "Sorry for making you remember..."

Therin pressed a kiss to the back of her hand. "The worst part about losing them was the time we missed out on together because of my job. Ironically, it was my job that took them away from me." His grip on her hand tightened. "So much wasted time."

"Well, then you and I—" she inched up to plant a kiss to his furrowed brow "—are just gonna have to promise to live and to not waste a second."

His smile emerged. "That's gonna be tough...we're a couple of in-demand folks, you know?"

"Tell me about it." She slapped his chest with a tuft of her hair. "Guess we're just gonna have to make the most of every stolen moment."

Therin gathered her close and rolled her beneath him. "Guess we should get started then."

They were in the midst of a glorious kissing and fondling session when the phone rang. It stopped when unanswered and then resumed.

"Remind me to find the off switch for that thing," Therin grumbled against Kianti's back when she moved to answer. Curiosity shimmered on his face when he heard her woeful groan.

"Hey, Mom..."

Therin took note of the change in her demeanor. She was almost childlike, subdued as she spoke with her mother. There was virtually no trace of the tough, take-no-prisoners woman he'd come to know so well.

"So when do I get to meet your folks?" he lightly inquired once the peculiar call had ended. "I just realized we haven't even talked about it." He tugged on a lock of her hair. "You're not ashamed of me, are you?"

She tried at a smile and failed. "Didn't want to make a point of discussing them when yours…"

He pulled her into a loose hug. "I love you for thinking of me, but don't you think I should meet them if we're going to be family? Unless you're waiting for us to meet up when your dad walks you down the aisle?"

She gave into laughter then, but it silenced all too soon. "What happened to your family isn't the only reason." She pushed up in bed and sat cross-legged in the middle. "My dad…he's very laid-back, a real easygoing kind of guy. My mom…she's another story. We love each other but the fact that I am who I am… Mom tends to go overboard with making sure *everyone* knows I am who I am when all I want is to hide out at home for a little TLC."

Therin's gaze narrowed as it softened. "Sounds like she's just proud of you. Could be worse, you know? She could treat you like an invalid." He winked.

Kianti's smile was sad. "That's part of it, too. 'Poor Kianti, it takes all of her strength to belt out such exquisite pieces. My baby's quite a marvel, isn't she?'"

"You're kidding?" Therin asked around his laughter.

"Unless I'm behind a piano, my mother doesn't want me doing anything." She laughed a little then. "My dad and I love to get away and fish but we have to sneak off to do it."

Therin was wiping laugh tears from his eyes by then.

"But fishing's one of the most restful— No?" He asked at the sight of her shaking her head.

"'Kianti shouldn't be out there in the hot sun or dead of winter trying to wrestle down some smelly fish,'" she quoted.

"I think we're just gonna have to educate your mom on what a strong kid she's got." Therin kissed his fiancée's cheek.

"Good luck. I can only pray you'll still want to marry me after meeting Francina Lawrence." Kianti's smile was barely there when Therin tugged her into a tight hug.

San Francisco, California~

Donald and Francina Lawrence were a lovely couple who seemed to complement each other quite well. Therin couldn't get past how much of them he saw in Kianti. They were all so very small, he felt like a veritable giant bowing humbly as he shook hands with his future in-laws.

Kianti kissed her father and then went to her mother for a hug.

"My Lord, Kibbie, he's a gorgeous thing, isn't he?" Francina whispered so only her daughter could hear.

"Ma." Kianti had never heard her mother go on with such awe. A genuine smile curved her mouth.

"We have to admit this is quite a surprise for us," Donald Lawrence said once the waitress at the Lark Garden headed off to fill their drink orders. "Kibbie told us she was seeing someone and now engaged…

We can see the love, though." Donald glanced toward his wife who nodded reverently.

"Sorry for springing this on you guys." Kianti watched Therin kiss the back of her hand. "Everything really did happen very fast."

"Therin, tell us more about what you do. My husband ordered me not to pry, but now I guess I'm allowed." She smiled bashfully. "A little," she added.

Kianti chuckled as Therin smiled and pressed a hand to the black-and-gray-spotted tie he wore. "Politics," she announced before he could say anything. "Therin's the former ambassador to Canada."

"Wait a minute," Donald breathed, following several silent seconds. "Rucker..." he closed his eyes as realization ensued. "I've heard of you. Education? The education organization, right? I'll be damned." He leaned over to shake hands with Therin again. "You lead a very interesting life, Mr. Rucker."

Therin bowed his head to accept the fact. "It's never been anywhere close to this interesting."

Kianti could see the change in her father's expression. "What is it, Daddy?"

Donald Lawrence reached out for his daughter's hand, squeezing it when she took hold. "I'm happy for you, Kibbie." His deep-set gaze was soft with love and pride, but clouded noticeably when he looked to Therin again. "You seem like a good man, but I've followed what news there's been about this. Is my daughter safe?" He set Kianti an apologetic look. "I'm sorry, baby, I have to ask."

"I understand that Mr. Lawrence—"

"It's Don and Francina, Therin. You're gonna be part

of the family." Donald nodded and leaned close to shake hands with Therin again.

"Sir." Therin smiled as if surprised by his reaction to Donald Lawrence's use of the word family. "I promise you she's safe. I'd give my life before I let anything happen to her." Blindly, he reached for Kianti's hand. "I don't suspect that'll be necessary, though." He smiled again, bringing much needed lightness to the moment.

Kianti pressed her cheek against his. "Thank God," she murmured, shivering contentedly when he held on to her.

"Someone I thought I could trust switched their loyalty to the other side…" Therin thought of Vaughn Burgess then. "But he's cooperating now and his people are pretty much running for cover. It's not the happiest of endings, but I'll take it. Especially if it means I get this woman for my wife." He kissed Kianti's cheek.

"An engagement like this…" Francina leaned back and fiddled with the rows of baby pearls nestled in the draping neckline of her rose-blush dress. "Honey, have you thought about what this means?"

Kianti laid a hand across her mother's. "It means we're in love."

Conversation silenced when the waitress approached the table with drinks and took dinner requests.

"There's so much to do." Francina sighed and sent a huge smile toward her husband. "I've got to call Sherrill's Florists. They did such a spectacular arrangement for the wedding of the daughter of one of your dad's associates. It was like a sea of—"

"Mommy? What are you doing?"

"Honey…" Francina regarded her only child as

if she'd lost her mind. "You are a renowned pianist. Therin's practically royalty…" Francina's lovely dark face was a picture of barely concealed glee. "This won't be a run-of-the-mill wedding."

"Whatever needs to be done, I'll handle." Kianti closed her eyes when her mother laughed.

"But that's crazy!" Francina tugged on the long wrist-hugging sleeve of Kianti's eggshell wrap dress. "You're in no condition for that, baby."

"Mrs. Lawrence?" Therin graced the woman with a smile that silenced her and brought a look of adoration to her eyes.

"I should tell you that your daughter isn't quite as fragile as she may have led you to believe." He shrugged a tad. "I should know since she saved my life a few weeks ago."

The Lawrences were indeed stunned. Silently, they listened intently as Therin shared the story of what had happened in North Dakota—what hadn't made it into the news broadcasts Donald had viewed. Still, it was a rather watered-down version. Therin left out the more grizzly elements but offered a pretty clear relay of the events.

Donald was quite impressed. Sadly, the story had the adverse effect on Francina.

"Well, I'd say that's about all the exertion you can handle, wouldn't you, Kibbie?"

"Mom, I—"

"It's settled then. For the next several days, weeks, or—" She took a breath at last. "Have you two even set a date yet?"

Therin was speechless, floored by Francina

Lawrence's elation. He looked over at Kianti who gave him an "I told you so" look.

Dinner arrived then. As everyone prepared to dig into the delicious-looking Asian feast, Francina pressed a reassuring kiss to her daughter's cheek.

"You just sit back, honey, and let me handle everything."

Therin barely managed to stifle his grunt when Kianti slammed her fist into his thigh.

The trip back to Pacifica was silent. Therin let it play out until they were inside the house, where he turned Kianti into his chest for a hug. She relished it, melting into the embrace the second his arms came around her.

"So do you still want to marry me now that I've been exposed as a wimp?"

He kissed the top of her head and squeezed her tight. "You're the sexiest wimp I've ever met, so I guess you're still stuck with me. I'm taking you to bed." He spoke softly against her ear and kissed her there as he carried her through the darkened house.

"Kia…" Therin began to rise from his slumber, stretching against the linens. "Kia?" He grimaced then realizing she wasn't there next to him or anyplace else in the room. The grimace he wore faded whilst curiosity set in. He heard music and decided to follow it.

The closer he came to the music, the deeper his curiosity grew. The phrases of the piano were beautiful, affecting and…pounding. The passion had an enraged edge. Therin could see why when he found her out on the balcony banging away. He waited until she'd stopped to catch her breath.

"You play hard to drive away the frustration, don't you?"

Kianti stilled but didn't look at her fiancé. "Does seeing my mother's face on the keys mean I'm disturbed?"

Therin grinned. "Maybe just a little." He sat behind her on the bench, pulling her back against his chest.

"And you *still* want to marry me?"

"More every second."

"I thought that 'Mom's face on the piano keys' comment may've been a deal breaker."

He turned her slightly on the bench to face him. "Nothin's gonna break this deal, Ms. Lawrence." With that said, he kissed her slowly.

The engagement party was put together in record time but it lacked no special touch. From the dazzling floral arrangements set amidst the fine antiques present throughout the Lawrences' enchanting Marin County home, everything was top-notch in the elegance department. When the guests of honor arrived, the frenzy reached its peak.

"I told her no press…" Kianti grumbled while her fingers curved deeper into the sleeve of Therin's eggshell jacket.

"You're a renowned pianist and I'm…practically royalty." He repeated her mother's words and grunted when she elbowed him.

"Ex," Kianti retorted.

"Anyway, we're world renowned. Press is a part of it."

"Hmph. Even if they want to grill you about everything that happened?"

"They don't know enough yet to grill me." Therin's easy expression tightened some as he studied the heavy crowd. "Besides—" he stroked the satiny brown skin between her shoulder blades bared by the V-cut back of her wine-colored dress "—they'll have a tough time getting anything out of me since I plan on kissing my fiancée on the dance floor all night."

"Why, Mr. Rucker, are you asking me to dance?" she drawled intentionally, laughing when he offered his arm.

"What do you think our chances are of talking my mom into a small wedding?" Kianti was asking once they were surrounded by a sea of slow dancers.

"World renowned…" Therin sang.

"Elopement…" she countered.

"Stop." He flexed his arm about her waist. "You'd break their hearts. You're their only child—only daughter at that. Don't you think Mr. Donald would want to give you away?"

She rolled her eyes. "Damn you for reminding me of that."

"Let me make it up to you."

The couple forgot all else and lost themselves in the dance and the sweet kisses that followed. Almost ten minutes passed before they were interrupted by one of the servers. Francina Lawrence wanted them for pictures.

"Is this a part of the only daughter's duty?" Kianti asked through her aggravation.

Therin shrugged. "I'm pretty sure it's in the good daughter's handbook."

The photo op lasted about twenty minutes. It seemed more like an hour to Kianti. The sight of familiar faces however, took her mind off any frustration.

"Lookin' good, Mrs. Ambassador," Cube was saying as he tugged her into a bear hug.

"We aren't married yet." Her voice was muffled against the sleeve of his dark jacket.

"Close enough," Khan said while pulling her back and kissing her cheek.

"You guys had better be there. No last-minute business," she ordered, poking a finger to the handkerchief peeking out of Winton's front pocket when he kissed her other cheek.

"We've waited a long time to find someone suitable to take you off our hands." Brody turned her to face him. "No way are we missin' this." He hugged her while the rest of the guys crowded around.

Therin chuckled at the scene they made. As he stood there watching the huddled group, an idea formed.

Kianti wanted to purr in response to the kisses showering her back. Content, she stretched against the covers, turned to her back and smiled up at Therin.

"What's up?" She took note of his clothing. "Great suit."

He smirked and brushed the edge of the mocha silk tie against her arm. "Just can't go to city hall lookin' shabby, you know?"

"City hall?" Her voice was a whisper and then she followed his bright gaze to the closet door. A gorgeous white suit hung there beneath a sheet of clear plastic. "For me?"

"Get dressed."

Kianti squealed, flung herself against his chest and planted a hard kiss to his mouth.

"Therin?" It was some time later when Kianti made her way toward the living room. She gasped, taking in the transformation of the corridor. "Therin?" Her voice had lost a bit of its strength.

He appeared then at the end of the lily-lined hallway. "Like I said, you just can't go to city hall looking shabby. But right about now, I'm thinkin' we look too damned good for city hall."

"What is all this?" she asked while he escorted her into the living room. Her second squeal of the morning carried across the room when she saw the guys there along with Vernon and Wren Shay.

"I was thinking," Therin spoke low as he hugged her close, "I'm a diplomat. I, of all people, should be able to come up with a solution that'd be pleasing to everyone, right?" With that said, he turned Kianti toward her parents.

Tears sparkled in Kianti's eyes when she saw them. Unashamed, she cried heavily into her father's suit coat when he tugged her close.

"You knew I'd have to give my baby away, didn't you, Kibbie?"

"I'm sorry, Daddy." She blinked away her tears

when he shushed her with a kiss. She looked over at her mother then. "Mommy, I—"

"Shh…it's time for *me* to apologize and, baby, I am sorry." Francina smiled adoringly while toying with the dark tendrils that hung in curls outside the high chignon atop Kianti's head. "I've never been very good at seeing what was right in front of me. So focused on that fragile, beautiful, gifted baby girl of mine, I almost missed out on seeing the beautiful, gifted woman she'd become. And she's strong as hell, too."

Kianti laughed amidst her tears.

"You think you can give your old lady another chance?" Francina's laughter resounded when her daughter pulled her into a powerful embrace.

"I've got quite a son-in-law here." Francina smiled over at Therin while she and Kianti hugged. "He's definitely got a talent for making people see the light."

Donald Lawrence leaned close and kissed his wife's cheek. "He's not our son-in-law yet, Franki," he playfully reminded her, and then straightened and offered his arm.

"Shall we?" he asked and then led Kianti to her fiancé.

The ceremony was quiet and lovely. Wren and Francina could be heard throughout the nuptials softly laughing or crying in happiness as the couple spoke their vows and were pronounced husband and wife.

The newlyweds spent their wedding night in Pacifica. The next morning they were scheduled to head out to begin their honeymoon. First stop: an uncharted island in the South Pacific.

Kianti left the bathroom to find her husband asleep in the armchair near the bed.

"A sign of things to come?" she asked, watching him fidget at the sound of her voice.

Therin yawned, but tuned in fast when he saw his wife standing naked before him. Her hair hung loose and thick about her like a dark frame.

Before he could leave the chair, she was settling down over him.

"Mmm-mmm…" She denied his attempts to lift her and squeezed his hands where they curved about her hips. She smiled when her nibbles to his earlobe and the graze of her breast against his chest caused him to melt beneath her. Only one area remained hard and un-yielding. She took full advantage. Torturing him slow, she rubbed her bare sex against the cottony soft fabric of his sleep pants. Impossibly, his shaft seemed to firm even more.

Therin moved to free himself, but Kianti pressed his hands to her chest instead. She moved seductively against him, arching her breasts into his palms and moaning soft when the nipples grazed there.

Mere seconds passed and then Therin was includ-ing his provocative mouth in the foreplay. Cupping one breast, he captured a nipple and suckled it into a glis-tening, firm nub of sensation. His thumb encircling the other nipple produced almost the same result. A few seconds of suckling and it produced the same glisten-ing quality.

Kianti was in danger of melting then herself. Pre-ferring to save a lengthier scene for later, she helped herself to what lay beneath Therin's pants. Tugging on a few snaps freed him instantly.

Therin let his forehead rest on her shoulder when she took him inside her and began to ride him slow. Kianti eased up and down the throbbing length of him, a sense of empowerment welling inside her each time he moaned in response. His nose trailed a path from her shoulder to the seductive rise of her bosom.

Massaging strokes to her back brought her closer to his mouth, nudging her nipples against the provocative curve of his lips. When he captured one, she ceased moving up and down his rigid shaft and rotated herself upon it.

Therin muttered a curse and captured her bottom in an unbreakable grip. Kianti threw back her head and let him take her as he would. He chanted her name harshly near the valley between her bosom. Every savage thrust stoked a groan from each of them. Kianti's hands fell away from Therin's broad muscular shoulders and she braced them to either arm of the chair while adding more force behind the surge of her hips.

Beautifully, they reached the plateau of satisfaction in unison. Content and in love, they shared the chair for a long time still intimately connected.

"Thank you," she murmured later as they cuddled in bed.

"For what?" Therin's deep voice was heavier against the desire she roused by gliding her mouth across his abs, which flexed gorgeously from the contact.

"For everything. Especially saving my life."

He smiled, eyes still closed in contentment. "I think you've got that backward."

"No," she moved over him. "No," she repeated when he opened his eyes. "In every way that matters, you saved my life. You gave me my mother." Her gaze faltered against the pressure of unexpected tears. "My entire life I don't think she ever saw me—never *really* saw me until this morning." Playful suspicion narrowed her tilting dark stare then. "What'd you say to them?"

Therin's mouth twisted into a lazy smirk. "The truth. What *really* happened in Neche. Told them about your pill strike." He tugged her hair when she looked away. "But I think it was what I shared about all of our stolen moments that gave them the truest insight into their little girl."

"Stolen moments," Kianti sighed. "Will our lives be made up of a series of those, I wonder?"

"Considering who we are...I'd say there's a serious chance of it." He nudged her chin with his fist. "Is that a deal breaker for you, Mrs. Rucker?"

Kianti grazed her lips along his jaw and then fixed him with a look that was both dazzling and devoted. "Nothing's gonna break this deal, Mr. Ambassador."

* * * * *

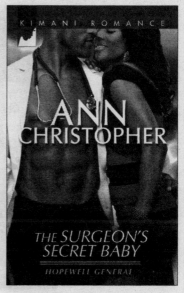

REQUEST YOUR FREE BOOKS!

2 FREE NOVELS PLUS 2 FREE GIFTS!

KIMANI ROMANCE ™

Love's ultimate destination!

YES! Please send me 2 FREE Kimani™ Romance novels and my 2 FREE gifts (gifts are worth about $10). After receiving them, if I don't wish to receive any more books, I can return the shipping statement marked "cancel." If I don't cancel, I will receive 4 brand-new novels every month and be billed just $4.94 per book in the U.S. or $5.49 per book in Canada. That's a saving of at least 21% off the cover price. It's quite a bargain! Shipping and handling is just 50¢ per book in the U.S. and 75¢ per book in Canada.* I understand that accepting the 2 free books and gifts places me under no obligation to buy anything. I can always return a shipment and cancel at any time. Even if I never buy another book, the two free books and gifts are mine to keep forever.

168/368 XDN FEJR

Name _____ (PLEASE PRINT) _____

Address _____ Apt. # _____

City _____ State/Prov. _____ Zip/Postal Code _____

Signature (if under 18, a parent or guardian must sign) _____

Mail to the **Reader Service:**

IN U.S.A.: P.O. Box 1867, Buffalo, NY 14240-1867
IN CANADA: P.O. Box 609, Fort Erie, Ontario L2A 5X3

Not valid for current subscribers to Kimani Romance books.

Want to try two free books from another line?
Call 1-800-873-8635 or visit www.ReaderService.com.

* Terms and prices subject to change without notice. Prices do not include applicable taxes. Sales tax applicable in N.Y. Canadian residents will be charged applicable taxes. Offer not valid in Quebec. This offer is limited to one order per household. All orders subject to credit approval. Credit or debit balances in a customer's account(s) may be offset by any other outstanding balance owed by or to the customer. Please allow 4 to 6 weeks for delivery. Offer available while quantities last.

Your Privacy—The Reader Service is committed to protecting your privacy. Our Privacy Policy is available online at www.ReaderService.com or upon request from the Reader Service.

We make a portion of our mailing list available to reputable third parties that offer products we believe may interest you. If you prefer that we not exchange your name with third parties, or if you wish to clarify or modify your communication preferences, please visit us at www.ReaderService.com/consumerschoice or write to us at Reader Service Preference Service, P.O. Box 9062, Buffalo, NY 14269. Include your complete name and address.

KROM11B

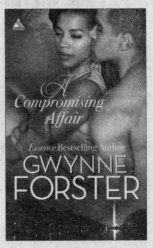

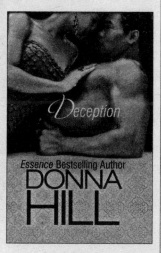